Fathers' Day

H J Brennan

Wing&
a Prayer
Books

This is a work of fiction. Names, characters, businesses, places, events, locales, and incidents are either the products of the author's imagination or used in a fictitious manner. Any resemblance to actual persons, living or dead, or actual events is purely coincidental.

For Veronica Muzic

The First Part

December 25, 2000: *Francis Danuta*

It was supposed to be Christmas. Francis Danuta sat on the raw wood floor, his legs extended with his back against the bed. Sneakers. Rotten sneakers. Who wore sneakers in the winter? He did. Francis Danuta, whose bastard of a dad was dead. Francis Danuta, only son of Isabel Danuta and only brother of Kathy Ann Danuta of Southern Avenue and member of the graduating class of 2001 who would never graduate and never marry and who stomped dirty, rotted sneakers through sidewalk slush wherever it was he thought he was going all winter long while anyone in their right mind was wearing those really warm—And waterproof!—boots from the sporting goods store that had all that cool stuff like baseballs and Barry Bonds signature gloves and tents and backpacks and hunting gear and fishing gear and bone-handled knives, and he could go in there and take just about one of everything—really cool stuff. That green canoe. Damn! It hung there from the ceiling waiting for someone like him— him and his Iroquois guide—to cut it down, slide it into the river and head out. Just him and—what's his name?

Hell, he didn't know—Gray Feather. Yeah, him and Gray Feather and their boots and Woolrich shirts and Coleman stove and Buck knives. They'd fish and hunt their way along the inland waters south, like maybe to Florida and meet up with some Seminoles, and Gray Feather could understand them, and they'd trade tobacco for supplies and just live there in the Everglades by Disney World.

The house was quiet. His mom left with the neighbor, Mrs. Griggs, and he should have gone with her, but he was sick, and she was like on autopilot, and it was all official business and forms, and please sign here, and she talked in spurts like bullets, and his chills were back. Don't say bullets. Besides, Mrs. Griggs made him crazy on a good day. But, she was a great neighbor and baking them a casserole and driving Mom to the hospital and all. They'd bring Kathy home tomorrow. God, she looked like shit.

What had he done?

What if he ran away? Somewhere like—Switzerland. They were neutral, right? Whatever that meant. He'd seen the pictures: hiking, skiing, eating and drinking at long wooden tables, and everybody was happy and rich. Like, everybody dressed for the snow and nobody—Nobody!— wore these fucking sneakers.

He'd been up all night and held it together pretty well until her pills kicked in, and his mom finally went to bed. She was talked out, and he was talked out, and they agreed to get some rest and deal with whatever comes next tomorrow. Lights off, he pulled her covers up to her chin, crossed the short hall to his room, closed the door and stood, hands at his sides in the screaming dark and waited for his insides to stop. They didn't, and, until an hour ago, he'd been throwing up—mostly clear stuff—into the toilet.

Mom said he had to go to the service, and it was for her that they were going, "If for no other reason!" She kinda put her foot down about that one—really pissed and, "I don't want to hear another thing, Francis! You're going!" He couldn't. She said it won't be for another week—the service. Kathy might be able to go, by then, but he couldn't. If he wasn't sick that day—which he probably would be—he'd say he was. He wasn't going, for sure.

Downstairs, the phone, again. "Hello, you have reached…" His mom's voice in a barrel, "…and have a nice day." *Beeeep!*

"Isy, you there? Isabel, you guys up? It's Bobby. We're gonna have to fingerprint the kids. Give me a call as soon as you can. Okay?"

Bobby. Uncle Bobby called. Fingerprints.

Francis got up and held onto the bedpost. His head. He had one light in his room—on his desk. It had been Bobby's wife's—Aunt Shirley's—when she was a kid. Porcelain. It was a small fancy coach attended by coachmen and pulled by four horses. He switched it on, and almost nothing changed. Over to the window, he released the blind. It snapped, wrapped around itself and—shit—he'd have to take it apart to get it to go back down. Everything out the window was gray: light gray, medium gray, black. Ripped plastic storm sheeting whipped against old glass. The window rattled. He looked down on the roof of a bus. *Whoosh!* The doors opened, and someone in a bright orange hunting cap stepped off, hurried a dozen steps up the walk through the storm and onto a porch. Frost on the panes, a little snow blew through the cracks and into the room.

Fingerprints. Uncle Bobby. What a life that guy had, like everything squared away, right? Even out of uniform he was all pressed and perfect: his cousins, Aunt Shirley, their house—friggin nice—up the hill from the creek and a new leather Grand Cherokee in the drive. That and the Mustang. He'd have that car, like whenever you want to give it away, Uncle Bobby, just say.

He was weak. Sweating.

Cold. It was always cold in his room, freezing. Kathy's room was the only one that was warm—above the kitchen.

His arms folded tight, and—"Aghhh!"—he fell onto the bed and wrapped in knots of blankets. He twisted into himself, fists jammed beneath his chin, and he shook. Cramps in his hands, his legs and feet, and the blankets were already soaked. He waited for it, and the ringing in his ears, and his teeth clenched, and it took for-goddam-ever until the warmth came to the bed and made it through his gut to his shoulders and hands and he was drained. He was done with it. There was just the storm and the dark at the window, and they faded and the shudder and the howl and the lamp on the desk and, for a while, it all stopped. His dead weight pressed deep into the mattress, and his coils unwound. He relaxed enough to cry, and, finally, to sleep.

Summer 1994: *Francis Danuta, aka, Frank and Frankie*

It was the summer between sixth and seventh grades that Francis Danuta saved his little sister Kathy's life. It wasn't until years later that they both thought of it that way: that Francis had saved Kathy's life. At the time, they both got into so much trouble for playing at the river— Kathy slapped hard and grounded for a month, and Francis with a broken thumb from his beating—that no one considered the day's events from a heroic angle.

That rolling Susquehanna was beyond Francis' sense of scale and place, and that its drowning currents were strictly off limits only sweetened its attraction. The river came from some greater unknown and far away where other kids probably wondered at its mystery just as he did. There were all kinds of stories around that river. He'd heard that up in farm country, ten years ago and somewhere near Lock Haven, a train went off the bridge, and all the crew was still trapped inside because it was too deep to retrieve the bodies, and once-in-a-while one of their hats, a glove or a shoe was found here along the banks. And, these banks. It was here, at this very spot, that hundreds of Indians—and they were Susquehannocks—had their village, and lived, and fished and raided forts and settlements all over the place.

The river was the kids' lodestar pulling them with all its timeless lore, an old man of a river knowing what has been and offering what was to be. They had but to step in.

And, they did.

The best access to the river was through Trumble's Lumberyard, as it was called. Other than its blanket of woodchips and sawdust giving up old bread smells, it wasn't a lumberyard at all, but a place where a thriving mill had once been, there along the river and back in the golden days of logging. What it really was, was a lot of rotted wood bracings struggling to support a huge, frozen saw blade, a rusted out '37 Ford panel body sunk into the wet earth and a few heaps of gray and checked rough-cut planks strewn about—so, it wasn't really a lumber yard at all. But, old man Trumble thought it was, and he still showed up every day in his McCulloch hat and Dickies bibs to oversee the past.

Two weeks ago at the river, they had tucked their bikes and shoes into the thick underbrush along the bank, and little Kathy balked. "I hate the mud. I really hate this part, the getting in and getting out."

They slipped in one after the other, Francis first and Kathy complaining behind.

"Shhh," Francis hissed. The mud sucked them in to just below their knees as they waded chest deep into the silent, gliding cool and doggy paddled twenty-five-yards crosscurrent to the first island. That's where old man Trumble's fifty-five-gallon oil drums were stored and all kinds of other great stuff for building rafts. Suffering a combination of scrapes and bruises and employing other such tactics, they were able to overpower the woven roots, twisted limbs and giant anacondas fortifying that shore and penetrate to the jungled island's interior.

"Over here!" Francis called, having found a very promising coil of rope. "This is gonna be good."

"Great," Kathy said. "Let's get the barrels."

This wasn't the first raft they built, but it would be their last. Actually only a few barrels loosely lashed together they would climb aboard and float so ever slowly, so triumphantly, a hundred yards downstream before grounding in the mud and abandoning in the late sun.

They'd been at this a couple years now and pretty much had it down: getting to the river and out to the islands. However, getting back to their bikes, and out of Trumble's yard without catching the old grouch's fury didn't always go so well. On their way in, dive bombing the lane and into the yard, they carried enough momentum to blitz into the undergrowth undetected. But, their laughter, splashing and the rest of the racket they made coming ashore and retrieving their bikes from the underbrush alerted the old man and gave him plenty of time to track them down and wait in ambush.

This time at the river, it was an especially hot, still day—the air thick—and little Kathy's mud whining prompted a hushed, shaded, riverbank discussion regarding alternative means of getting to the island.

"I'm not getting sucked into that mud again," Kathy whispered. "Can't we just float out on a couple boards? Maybe go further upstream and see if it's rocky?"

"Right," Francis said, scanning the treetops. "And we can leave our bikes up there in old man Trumble's driveway. Maybe Mrs. Trumble will watch them for us. Check those cables."

"Huh?" Kathy asked.

"There's those two cables, one above the other, that run from that pole at Trumble's and out to the island."

"And, what?"

"Those big cables run right through those trees, there. We shinny up a tree and side step on the bottom cable and hold onto the top one and cross the water."

On the way to Trumble's yard, they'd pedal past The
Sweet Shop and Deacon's Sporting Goods. On mission,
the kids never stopped on their way to the river, but, once
in a while on their return trip, they'd pop into The Sweet
Shop for an ice cream. And, once and only once, they'd
been inside Deacon's. They'd left their bikes leaning on
the wall at The Sweet Shop and crossed the road to
the Sporting Goods with their single scoops dripping. In
the window, a stuffed grouse, a ten-point buck and a
fearsome wolverine were displayed with an assortment of
complicated spotting scopes and a fanned array of Buck
knives. Behind the display was a large framed photograph
of a hunting party with its packs and rifles and big game
trophies gathered on the dock in front of a sea plane in
Alaska, and that was the short, wide and bundled, Deacon
himself right there in the middle. Kathy peered in through
the screen door and whispered, "Uuhhh, look!" Francis
scuttered around her and saw it: the biggest polar bear
ever, there in the back corner of the store, reared up to its
full height, claws raised and baring its long, man-eating
teeth. They left a couple flavors on the door handle as they
were drawn silently in, creeping around to the left like
feral cats past the knife case, the hats and flannel shirts,
toward that bear. Kathy was first to arrive at the beast,
just knee high, and, as in a trance, she reached out a
pistachio'd hand. Behind them, a voice exploded.

"Who the hell let you in here?! Do you little nitwits
have a mother? Is she nuts letting you run around without
a collar? You've probably got rabies! Get the hell out of
here before I call the pound!"

They froze.

"What, are you deaf, too? Get the hell outta here before
I shoot your skinny asses and hang you on the wall!"

They hit the screen door in a dead heat, nearly tearing
it from its frame, and were on their bikes and peddling
hard for home as the pudgy, grinning Deacon waddled
over and checked the door hinges.

They'd decided Francis would be first to climb to the cables and cross to the island, then Kathy. Francis leaped, grabbed hold of the lowest limb, pushed against the trunk with one foot, pulled himself up onto the branch and landed softly on his butt. He extended a hand to Kathy. "Next?" Once Kathy was aboard, Francis laddered up a few more limbs and was out onto the cables, tentative, slow, the strands much more flexible and goosey than he'd imagined. It got worse once Kathy was on them. Near the middle and sagging twenty feet above the water, it was impossible, with the upper cable being of one purpose and the bottom having a different plan entirely. Francis found himself nearly face down horizontal a couple times.

"Wait, Kathy. Just stay there til I'm closer to the other side. Don't move."

The water had turned a deep, eerie green and showed tiny whitecaps with the wind coming up. Francis welcomed the relief of the breeze, though it might complicate this squirrely crossing. The rolling skies emitted a distant summer rumble, and it looked like rain, but they'd be getting soaked today, anyway. So what? He continued across, got close enough to the other side where the cables were steady and called, "Okay. C'mon, Kathy, we don't have all day."

The cable sways increased as the wind rolled in. Kathy edged near the middle and stopped. "I can't!"

"Kathy, it's easy, c'mon! I'll meet you out there." Francis started back out. "C'mon, now."

Kathy took quick baby side steps and went hand-to-hand, hand-to-hand. "Frankie, go back!" she said in tears. "You're making it swing. Go back right now!"

Keeerack! A bolt of lightning cratered the water, split Kathy's T-shirt and threw her small body spread-eagled backwards fifteen feet into the dark river. Francis stutter-blinked. Mute shock and disbelief, and it rained pitch forks. Francis dove, submerged and arrived next to Kathy who floated limbs akilter and unconscious. One hand under Kathy's chin, Francis pulled with his free arm and kicked and pulled and kicked and pulled and dragged Kathy ashore as she slowly revived, moaning, her hair singed short. Leaving their bikes and shoes, Francis carried Kathy piggy-back through the downpour, up and out of the brush and across the lumberyard. Behind them—a muted voice in the rain—Francis was barely aware of old man Trumble's stick-flailing, "I told you so!"

That Same Summer, 1994: *Victoria Merritt Leaves Home*

Victoria Merritt's mom slipped Pop's lighter into her hand as she was about to board the bus and head off to college. It was a just-awakening Harrisburg morning when birds nestled shoulder-to-shoulder on silent phone lines, and by the still-radiant pavement, you knew this was going to be another scorcher. There in the parking lot with her mother, between moments, together and apart, she could smell the terminal's restrooms through the shuddering noise and exhaust of the towering row of buses. The bus for Elmira was full. The uniformed driver at the wheel fumbled in the dark with his thermos and patience. Last to board, Victoria turned on the narrow step for a quick glance at her mother. Her mom grabbed her hand, palmed the Zippo and gave her parting advice, "Keep your eyes open, listen up and accent the positive."

Blindly making her way down the aisle, her thighs bounced from armrest to mumbling passenger, left and right, as the Greyhound wove through the parking lot. Brakes whooshed, and she spun and stumbled onto her hands. Corduroy. There in the dark, the aisle felt like gritty rubber corduroy. The draft beneath the seats was a complex bouquet of congealed fast food, broken down Nikes and dirty laundry. Embarrassed, she again wondered if she belonged—at her place in the biological swirl. Were all the nameless people on this bus in on something she had missed? Had there been a passengers' meeting, an announcement just before her mother and she arrived at the terminal, something about seat assignments, a layover, a missing piece of information of the like that had, in the past, found her standing in the wrong lines at the DMV and class registrations? All the people on this bus made it here on time and had found seats of their choosing. Some were already asleep. She was on her hands and knees on the floor. She wondered at her chances of a fresh start at college, of being accepted, perhaps even embraced by a scholarly society. Her recent honors and scholarships were the last in a series of accolades she'd received over the years that her classmates found meaningless. It was all the things she couldn't do they found fascinating. She couldn't throw a ball, for instance. Nor, could she dance. Her mother gave lessons in their living room on a piano once played by Liberace, but Victoria couldn't play or sing. Her thoughts went to Pop and the lighter. She stuck it into her pocket as the bus lurched onto the street.

"Here," a child's voice from above.

Victoria gripped an armrest, found her feet and rose unsteady in the shifting dark. The aisle seat was unoccupied but for a backpack, a few bags and a jacket. The girl in the window seat moved her things to the floor. Victoria collapsed into the seat and exhaled. "Thank you."

"Fell, huh?"

"Yes. I sometimes struggle with the physical world." She brushed off her knees. "I'm Victoria, by the way." She turned and offered her hand.

The girl stared at her through the blinking dark, then faced forward. She took up almost no space, her entire body curled into the narrow seat. The passing lights strobed on a bronze silhouette, perhaps ten, twelve-years-old, with chopped black hair and bizarrely red lipstick.

Dawn at its starboard side, the bus broke through the city limits and gained momentum north against the current of the Susquehanna River.

Victoria reached up for the light, dug a paperback from her bag and wedged a leg beneath her into a somewhat acceptable position. The girl plugged in. Victoria's breathing relaxed to a slow rhythm, scanning left to right. Thirty pages down the road, she emerged from her concentration aware of new sounds: swishy music from the girl's ears, staccato shuffling of playing cards, laughter from a couple seats back and heavy tires at speed. She turned off the light.

"What are you listening to?"

The girl pulled a black plug from her head. "What?"

"Your music, what do you like?"

"None of it."

"But—"

"I listen to learn what they're thinking." She held the ear bud toward Victoria, "Right now, it's Third Eye Blind. They're new."

"Do you read?"

"What?"

"Sorry, I mean, for fun, you know? What do you like to read?"

"I don't know. Anything. Cereal boxes, street signs, Sartre."

"Really."

"Yeah."

"Sartre?"

"Yeah?"

"Well, some find his ideas bleak—challenging."

"Um."

"Well, I think it's pretty great that you read Sartre."

"And, I think it's great you think that."

"What else have you read?"

"I saw Spot run." She plugged back in.

The bus slowed and rocked side to side as it pulled into a convenience store at Port Treverton. Fresh mowed lawns and diesel exhaust sucked into the aisle as the doors opened, and a handful of wrinkled passengers unfolded, stood and debussed. The girl watched them through the window: some greeted by what looked like husbands, wives, grandparents and some just shuffled off alone into the bugs and heat. The girl's breath hit the glass, "You could get out here, right now, and your life would never be the same."

"Yes, but why?" Victoria asked.

"Why not?" Still to the window. "You think your life will go as planned? Has it so far? Really? What are you thinking? College?"

"I'm on my way to Syracuse."

"A rich husband, like maybe a doctor? A cool car, big TV and a pool? Kids?"

"Perhaps."

"A kid like me?" She turned to Victoria.

"I really don't know you, other than you read cereal boxes and Sartre."

Green eyes bored into her for an uncomfortable moment, then turned back. "You won't meet a doctor. It'll be the opposite."

"Excuse me?"

"Never mind."

A trio of hefty passengers clambered aboard wrestling packages, bags and a couple fussing toddlers. The bus swayed with their struggles.

They would be the opposite of what she envisioned. The girl was right. If she got off this bus here, in this little hamlet, and took up life as a, a, what? "And you are staying on this bus because?" Victoria asked.

"I'm going to my aunt's."

"How nice, then, a visit."

The girl spun back to the window. "Right."

"Will you be staying long?"

"Looks that way."

"I'm sorry? You don't—"

"My dad's moving back to the old country—the devil he knows. I was supposed to go, but I threw a fit and he put me on this bus."

"Which country?"

"Albania. We're Roma."

"Roma?"

"Outcasts. Dogs."

"I don't understand."

"Me neither. Just the way it is."

"And, your mother—she's here?"

"She never made it this far. I gotta get some sleep." She knotted up.

The doors closed, the brakes eased and the bus rolled back onto the highway.

She'll miss her father, Victoria thought. Misses him already. Images of the church, her mother's fists, her father's hat flashed at her. "He'll be back. Your dad loves you—sending you to be safe with your aunt. He'll be back." From the clutch of a girl, she heard a small cough.

"Wake up." The girl poked Victoria's shoulder.

"What? I'm sorry?"

"We're here, my aunt's town."

"Of course. You're going to your aunt's. She's meeting you here?"

"Nah, but it's cool."

Good grief, she thought. Is there no end to her? She's barely twelve. At eleven or twelve, well, she wouldn't have been on a bus by herself. "Shall we call her to pick you up? I could help, there's a short layover."

"She doesn't drive, and I'll find my way." She faced the front and folded her arms. "Look, Vic, you seem nice enough, and all, but we're from different planets, so you can just stop trying, okay? You're going to Syracuse where you'll start a reading group, work in a fabric store and graduate with honors, and I'm going to be on the other side of this river in my aunt's little alley apartment, going to a stupid new school, avoiding stupid new friends."

"A fabric store. Really. I don't even know your name."

"Tina Liberty."

"That's your name?"

"Yeah?"

"That is a very cool name."

The girl turned to her. "How old are you?"

"I'm eighteen."

"And, you think my name's Tina Liberty?"

Victoria slumped. "Oh. You must have a hard life."

The girl turned back to the window. "That'd be close to right. I'm Faye."

August 2000: *Faculty Orientation*

A week before school, her first department meeting and first impressions. Would the other teachers like her? Victoria leaned over the sink, dabbed a tissue at her face and took a deep air-conditioned breath. It had been a long warm trek from the metro bus up the hill, past the custodian hosing down the front steps and into this brand new high school. In the ladies' room, she wiped down her forearms and neck, fanned out the bottom of her blouse, wafted cool air beneath and ran a brown paper towel at her armpits, belly and chest. Another glance at the mirror found her black braid intact, and the make-up had held to her olive complexion. Best not to touch that. She retrieved her shoulder bag from the hook, pushed out through the heavy door and followed the colorful signs directing faculty to their meeting rooms.

The school was designed with little need for stairs, just endurance. Her meeting was in the language suite, and she'd been following the signs for nearly a quarter mile from the main entrance. She slowed her steps and approached the open door to her department's meeting. Inside, veteran teachers, having parked their cars close to that suites entrance, were well into their second or third coffee and pastry. A bit harried and close to late, she reset her clock for calm and entered.

At the front of the room, two tall, middle-aged men in slacks and polo shirts were losing the battle to plant a large contrary easel at the front of the room. A smaller, sweaty, curly-haired man in a garish Hawaiian shirt hunched over a tangle of orange extension cords behind the desk. The rest of the room was a summer backyard cacophony of, *he said...then she said...and then they... and Oh-my-God!* Victoria's arrival was ignored. She took a "Take One" folder from a blue stack near the front and headed for the last desk in the first row. She pulled the bag off her shoulder and hung it over the back of the chair. Her hands rested there, her fingers tapping no known rhythm as she hovered for a moment taking in the room, waiting—hoping—for someone, anyone, to glance her way. Okay, then, they hadn't. She sat.

Hands crossed on the desk, she measured the crowd. They milled about, everyone rapid-fire talking and no one listening, mostly youngish women, a few older than her mom. At the front of the room, one of the tall men at the easel had reached his limits of cooperation. "Goddammit, let me do this!" The other man raised both palms, tugged at his collar and whisked from the room in sockless loafers. He had a great tan.

Victoria fingered the corner of the folder. Dare she open it? She took another look around the room confirming she was invisible and opened to a cover sheet. It was a welcome message from the department chair she'd briefly met in the principal's office last spring during her second interview. The woman had stopped in just long enough to see for herself that Victoria was, in fact, human, stretched her lips in a tortured, saw-toothed smile and left. This year's welcome message to her department was nearly as warm:

Department:

In the following pages, you will find today's agenda, assorted worksheets, amendments to the state's core academic standards and an innovative lesson format and evaluation matrix I developed during my residency with Dr. Richard Ciganko at New Paltz this summer. I am sure you will find these last two documents to be especially helpful as you strive to increase your efficacy.

Sincerely,

Dr. Allison Fury, Chair, English Department

cc: Dr. Ronald Tannic, Superintendent
William Howard Hill, M.Ed., Principal

As the department settled in, there were thirty-plus seats for fourteen teachers and she was buffered by empties. She considered moving. Too late.

"Ladies and gentleman, and I know you, so you can take that as a compliment or an insult." It was the short sweaty guy in the Hawaiian fish shirt. "Welcome to the great bloody halls of Heorot and our struggle to bring literacy to the children of Grendel. Before we get into today's agenda, I am sorry to report that Dr. Fury will not be joining us."

Saccharin songs of sorrow swelled the room.

"Yes, I know, but we shall continue in her name."

"I thought she only had an adjective and a title!" someone said.

"Ahem," the fish shirt continued. "One other announcement. We welcome a new member to the department, a recent Syracuse graduate—graduate summa cum laude. Victoria Merritt will be conducting a section of Junior-Senior English and an honors class. Let's welcome Ms. Merritt." He led the tepid claps. A few teachers turned to stare. One, a heavy woman with short-cropped grey hair grinned widely and winked. The rest didn't bother.

The temperature seemed to have risen a few degrees. A blunt something repeatedly stabbed her between the eyes, and her neck pulsed. She pressed sweating hands into her lap, and this was her reception? This was the reception from her professional peers? She took a few calming breaths as the fish shirt continued from the front of the room. Okay, she had big expectations, so full of herself. Her big deal, not theirs. What did they care about some rookie who's never had her own class and hasn't had to deal with all the problems they've seen time and again? Most of them looked as though they'd been at it for years—this job. For them, it was just another day at work.

They had their folders open, and the shirt enjoyed himself with his oratorical gestures and intonation as he read the welcome message aloud. He was oddly hairy, now that she had a better look. He wore a loose gold watch.

She wouldn't let it be just a job. She'd show them by example, show them how important, how vital they were. She'd heard about this apathy creep at school, at Syracuse.

In her own classroom after the meeting, she adjusted her chair and stared out across thirty-two empty desks, barren shelves and sealed cartons of books and supplies. So, that was her first department meeting, and what did she learn? Either she had been foolish and naive, or this department didn't appear to try very hard, or care very much. She was not going to be very popular. She'd wrapped two donuts in a napkin and brought them back with her, and she didn't even *like* donuts. She bit into the maple glazed.

Leaning onto her forearms, she considered the monthly planner that consumed sixty-percent of her desk. Potential energy, she thought. Inert, inactive, at rest. Thirty September squares awaited her plans, reminders, things to follow up on the next day, quizzes, tests, grade deadlines, library and TV events, guest lecturers—she intended to bring in authors, poets, and playwrights—book reports and holidays.

"A little me time before the storm?"

Victoria jerked from her thoughts. The heavy, gray-haired woman leaned in. Her hands gripped both sides of the doorway.

"Yes, I—"

"It'll all hit the fan in a couple days, and it looks like you have a lot of work to do between now and then." The woman swaggered in, elbows splayed and hands stuffed in the back pockets of bagged-out madras shorts. Her bare knees grimaced like pug snouts.

"Yes, I hadn't realized—"

"Hits ya like a ton of bricks, your first week. There you are, thinking you'll just show up in your shiny new classroom and commence with years of cerebral bliss, and doe-eyed students admiring every ridiculous bead of half-truth you string. But, first come days of prep and shoring up before you even begin, and you have no idea how draining it is. No one does, what, with all the unpacking, sorting, arranging, student supplies, teacher supplies, setting up your files, grade books, emergency forms, resource materials hung—if you're so inclined—lesson plans tidied up. You have your lesson plans, right? Multiple copies: department, office, substitute plans and your own? That'd be five days a week and every day of the year. They ever teach you *that* at Syracuse? Also, empty cartons have to be broken down and stacked in the hall. You going to eat that donut?"

"No, I—"

"Thanks, gotta fuel the beast."

"I'm Victoria. I'm new to—"

"Yeah, we heard all about you in the meeting. So, anyway, welcome and I hope you make it. It's a long haul to the Christmas break. I work three doors down. If ya need anything, don't ask; we all have problems." She licked her fingers and wiped them on her shorts. "You're pretty much on your own around here. The department's chair, Queen Fury, is rarely on site—sailing the royal barge off to conferences to pick up her next award. And, if you turn to Little Howie for help—that'd be the principal— well, you'll only do that once. Word of advice: use Fury's new lesson plans and evaluation matrix. Hell to pay if ya don't."

"Thank you, I—"

"Nice chatting. Gotta get back to work." Mid-stride and half way out the door she called back, "I suggest you get your ass in gear!"

September 2000: One Week Later

The first school morning, Victoria had rolled over one last time and surrendered a sleepless night to the predawn. Sheets tortured, pillow spent, she pulled on her robe and padded out to start the coffee. Shower, hair, make-up sans lipstick, she poured a cup, dropped a slice into the toaster and pulled Mom's strawberry jam from the pantry shelf. Toast popped, jam spread, she sat at the small kitchen's table alternately spinning her lighter and flipping pages of *The Times*. An article jumped out. Anything about *The Yankees* would. 2000 was their one-hundredth season as a team, ninety-eighth in New York. Their pitcher, Andy Pettitte, had visited a convalescent hospital in Brooklyn. Nice guy, that Pettitte. All the rest of the paper was politics and money.

The lighter was a Zippo from back in the day—her grandfather's—the soft, chamfered edges rounder now than in the Pacific. The black finish remained only in the center of its flat, U.S.M.C. inscribed surface. Steel showed through at the edges. Cold, it warmed quickly to the palm and gave off the pleasant stinging scent of fuel and sixty years' proximity to tobacco. She planned to quit smoking today. That was her plan: to quit on her first day in the classroom. It would be a heroic act of self-improvement, a benchmark on her new life as a teacher and role model. She checked the clock and determined there was time for another.

Hours later, and facing live fire at the head of the classroom, Victoria Merritt is steeled. Back straight, shoulders square, she is confidence in black and white. Her first ever students pour through the door and scatter like BB's between rows of empty desks, and, in seconds, the room is surrendered to a barrage of rabid percussion. Books slam, chairs rattle, voices collide and career like grapeshot and the young, first-year teacher clears her throat. "Hello, and welcome."

Her face hints at Greek: plumb lips, dark, almond eyes. Black, size-eight and pleated Ann Taylor slacks, white blouse and a thin gray vest, she resets her jaw, raises her five-feet-nine another quarter-inch in already-painful heels and says a bit louder, "Class?"

She has arrived. This is her moment to step forth as an adult, an example—her time at the lectern to lead examinations into the humanities, the romances, the arts and letters—an example to these fledglings emerged from the crippling storms of puberty. She scans the chaos of the room and it is apparent: no one gives a damn.

They are crazy at this age, aren't they—hormones haywire, flying as possessed through the school parking lot in their parents' two-ton SUVs, smoking, toking, drinking and God knows what they've touched and whether they've washed their hands? Her gaze stops at the one squeezed into that skirt. Vital, sprung like a cat, alert breasts in tight polyester and did she save any mascara for tomorrow?

In the off-leash bedlam, the noise has risen to a level that may soon bring the principal to her door. She reaches into her toolbox and pulls out shock and awe. "McDonald's!" she calls out.

A guppy of a kid in the front row looks up and gulps. "Huh?"

She lowers the class roster to her desk behind her, takes a step closer to the shrinking lad and drills, "Why is it called McDonald's?"

He shrugs. "I dunno. Cause they sell burgers?"

"Good try. I might have guessed the same, but that's not it."

The room quiets. Rubberneckers slow for the carnage. A grinning boy plunked cross-legged on a desktop in the middle of the room challenges, "What was the question?"

She looks up and there they are, her first ever students parked on windowsills, desktops or standing in groups, most eyes fixed on her.

"I just asked this young man, and I apologize to you, sir, that I do not yet know your name, 'Why is McDonald's called McDonald's?'"

"Easy," he laughs. "Ronald McDonald."

She drifts down his aisle.

"Hmm, you mean there was this clown, Ronald, and, for some yet to be established reason, he was the start of the biggest restaurant chain in the world? Does everyone think that's pretty much how it happened?"

They find their seats.

"Burgers and fries in China, Korea, Argentina, Sweden, France and sub-Saharan Africa because there was a clown?"

Pause.

"Your first assignment—"

Moans.

"Your first assignment, due at this time tomorrow and five-percent of your semester grade: write one tight, fifty-to-one-hundred-word paragraph, and tell me why it's called McDonald's. Oh, and a five-point bonus if there's a woman involved. Spelling counts."

An article in today's *Times* reported the chain's heiress would be leaving a couple million dollars to public radio.

"Please find your English Literature books in your newly acquired stack. They're large, green and black. Place them, alone, on your desks; the rest can go below your seats." Victoria waited. "Now, please open your large green and black books to page 42 as I take roll."

The alert breasts in the white polyester belonged to Anne Marie Delucchi, and Anne Marie was sex in heated oil. A chipped tooth and reptilian brain put a wicked smile on that girl, and she could singe an ear with a whisper. Rumors surrounded the nineteen-year-old like fruit flies: college guys fought over her, she dated even older men, she'd ruined more than one marriage, and Anne Marie, loving the attention, did nothing to dissuade them.

The school was central Pennsylvania working-class populated by white protestants and Catholic ethnicity: Miller, Strauss, Bower and Afalani, Agnone, Carducci, Casherra Cellini, Delucchi, DiCanio, DeGreggori, Devito, Gnoffo, Mazzante, Miele, Molino, Musheno, Novielo...

The Polish were equally represented in the graduating class of a-hundred-and-fifty, and Anne Marie, behind her foot-high stack of books, and not having heard anything about a green and black literature book or page 42, had just leaned across the aisle and passed a note to Monica Chalupa.

The diminutive kid Victoria had confronted in the first row was Donald Mahonski. He would die that year barely leaving a space. Leukemia.

The boy on top of his desk who had offered the Ronald McDonald solution, now seated properly, was Francis Danuta, aka Frank and Frankie. Francis was a C student, capable of more, but unmotivated. He was not what you'd call handsome but good-looking, slender and just above medium height. He kept his clothes clean and pressed, but wore them long beyond their expiration dates and his shoes—the color of a washed-out road—well, all they said was, poor. The girls liked dancing with Francis. He was polite, cool and stayed in the moment. Another way of putting it would be that the boy lacked predatory ambition where any other guy would have been thinking, back seat of the Bronco, halfway through the first eight bars. Easily swept up with the crowd, like sitting on the desk just then, he was wrapped in the retreating sadness of an abused pet. His eyes slanted slightly down at the corners, and, most times, it was hard to tell if he was laughing or crying. The only trouble he'd ever had at school was when he intervened in a lopsided fight. A frequently-flunked senior named Bomber Hazzard had thrown a freshman into the lockers and was mopping up the floor with him. When Francis stepped in on behalf of the freshman, Hazzard turned on Francis and stomped him up one side and down the other until the teachers showed up. A scar bisecting his left eyebrow postmarked the event. Simple and pure, he was easily embarrassed and often blushed. Other than that one time with Hazzard, no one pressed things very far with Francis. Even the jocks thought it was too easy. In just a few months, he would try Victoria's soul.

Victoria checked the roster. "Anne Marie, will you please read our text aloud to the class, the second paragraph on page forty-two. Anne? Anne Marie?"

Anne Marie, her head darting from side-to-side, responded to the whispered coaching from her classmates and she:

1. found the book, "The green and black one!"
2. rifled pages to forty-two and
3. looked up to the front of the room, proud of her speedy recovery, smiled her evil smile and awaited further direction.

"The second paragraph, Anne Marie. Would you please read it aloud for the class?"

Behind all of the quest myths there seems to be a story of the universal quest of all men for their lost, true inheritance. Man begins his perilous journey to regain what he once had but has lost, guided by only a dim memory, kept alive in his imagination.

September 2000: *Francis' First School Night as a Senior*

"Where you going, Frankie? You have homework," Kathy sneered from the stairs.

"What?" he said into the mirror at the front door. He re-buttoned the top button.

"You know. That new teacher—the whole school knows. She assigned homework the first day."

He grabbed the doorknob. "Did not. Bye."

"Mom!"

He backed a step, closed the door and hissed, "Do you have to?"

"You gotta do it before you go out. I always have to, but I don't *have* homework." She stood as ceremoniously as her sixteen years would allow and descended noisy stairs to the front room like she was the Queen of the Prom, tripped at the frayed rug, regained, grinned back over her shoulder and pulled the door closed behind her.

He waited half-a-minute, giving her time to get to the corner, then he opened the door and—

"Francis? Do you have homework?" his mom called from the kitchen.

"Mah-uhm!" He closed the door and turned.

"Frankie?" His mom came into the front room—swollen lip, the floral bruise at the corner of her mouth.

"It's not really homework. S'posed to write why it's McDonald's. Makes no sense."

"Why what's McDonald's?"

"The burger place."

"We don't have one." She lightly touched her lip. "Other side of the river."

"See what I'm saying?"

September 2000: *Victoria's First School Night*

Shoulders rounded, Victoria carried her shoes and flatfooted up the three freshly-painted, broad wooden steps to the porch, made it around to her side entrance, opened the screen door, slipped the key into the deadbolt, twisted, shoved and stumbled into her apartment. She dropped her bag, flipped those shoes to the floor and collapsed into the couch. If she'd had a husband or a roommate, she'd have called out for a drink; a glass of wine would be perfect, a soothing merlot. That or a frosty Sam Adams and a smoke. It would have to wait. Husband? Hardly. She'd dated a few times at Syracuse; it had gone nowhere. She found herself cast in the role of coached audience *(APPLAUSE!)* for the extroverted boys as they sailed high on their self-involvement. On dates with the more cerebral, introverted types, she felt somewhat like steamed broccoli—a necessary part of a good diet recommended by their mothers. She had pretty much turned the page on dating. She hadn't anyone who cared, and she wasn't about to get up from the couch anytime soon. Out of order, there by the door, she considered those shoes. Were they designed to keep women chaste, so focused on their foot and lower back pain that straying thoughts were crushed at inception? Unbuttoning and unbridling, she sank back into the cushions and gave exhaustion full reign from her ankles to the base of her skull. There was a soft, late afternoon traffic rhythm that soon synchronized with the ticks of the kitchen clock, and the traffic and the clock...

> Her parents were sitting across from her at the table, and
> They ate in the kitchen. It was warm from the stove.
> The chicken steamed and smelled of rosemary and thyme, and
> Their knives and forks clicked on the plates.
> Her mother said, "Victoria, go to the church and get your father."
> "He's sitting there next to you, Mom."
> "Do as I say, Victoria."
> Then, he was gone.

She woke in the dark with a stiff neck, a dry mouth and feeling one size larger. All the blood had settled into her hands and feet. She rolled to her side, pulled up and out of the couch and stubbed her toe on the way to the kitchen. Damn, stove clock glowed 8:30, and she'd slept three hours. She snapped the light switch, put a pot on and leaned back against the counter. There was a lot of preparation for tomorrow, and, when she was done, she'd probably never fall back to sleep. Thank God there was just tomorrow, then the weekend. Whoever thought Thursday was a great idea for the first day of school was clairvoyant. The kids had challenged and tested her every moment, but it went better than she'd expected, not a total loss. She reached over to the table, grabbed the pack and tapped out a smoke. Time to get to work.

She had moved into this small, high-ceilinged, first floor apartment just a couple weeks ago and had done what she could to make it her own. The house was an undistinguished, early-century, clapboard two-story in a two-mile row of tired, single family homes and duplexes lining both sides of Southern Avenue. On one side of the house was the Southern Grill, and, if she didn't like their company or music, there was the neon cactus sign of the Southwestern Grill just three doors down on the other side of the street. Slate sidewalks lined the avenue running the length of the neighborhoods from the steel-arched bridge, past an ice-cream shop, the fire house, four schools, two barber shops, the beer distributor, two ball fields, five sub shops, a single hole-in-the-wall Chinese restaurant, four churches, eight bars, another ice cream shop and Derrick Brothers Used Cars to the other steel bridge and dead-ended at the concrete block plant and swamp. If you were looking for a library or a movie theater, you had to pick a bridge.

Coffee stirred, and lighting another smoke, she skimmed down the hallway to the bathroom. She hit the switch and was, as ever, amused by the mirror. This time it was Cubism from the midway: one cheek a major interchange of red creases, hair flattened to the same side and her lipstick a whimsical smear.

"Phew, good one," she said to the artist, taking a drag and tilting her head for a sideways glance. "Very special."

December 2000: *Pre-Holiday Open House and Parents' Night*

Victoria stood in the doorway and viewed her classroom as entering parents would see it an hour from now. First, of course, her desk; orderly and centered, it sat as the mother ship at the head of the five-row fleet of student desks. Aside from her laptop, a tiny, ebony-handled brass bell and a hand-thrown and salt-fired ceramic vessel holding spare pens and freshly-sharpened pencils, the surface was pristine. She had stashed today's ungraded papers into her bag and the desktop monthly planner was stored behind the low, freestanding bookcase at the back of the room; no need for parents to see her personal notes. Student written works hand-picked from each of her classes were laid on the desks. Row five displayed six comparative analyses of Shakespeare and Marlow from her honors class. As they entered her room, parents' attention would likely be drawn to the back expanse of whiteboards upon which Victoria had taped six poster-sized printouts of the Pennsylvania Core Curriculum Standards which, presumably, served as a beacon to every public English class in the state. She hoped the giant graphics would quickly inform parents regarding what was driving her efforts and what they could expect their kids to gain during their time with her:

CRITICAL THINKING: interpret, analyze, synthesize
ACTIVE LISTENING: question, reflect, respond, evaluate
EFFECTIVE SPEAKING: communicate addressing audience
EFFECTIVE RESEARCH: use varied resources
RULES of GRAMMAR: support clarity of communication
EXPANDED VOCABULARY: enhance ability to express

As she considered the standards, a nagging side thought—a stain—appeared. Small, at first, it grew. Was there a leak in her evening's plan? Difficult to place, the sound of the feeling within her. *Drip.* She felt incomplete, as if parts had been improperly assembled, and they weren't going to hold. Somewhere a leak. *Drip.* She swiveled her focus from the whiteboard, cocked her head and listened. She checked the clock. The first parents would be showing up soon and, *Drip.* She found it, the leak. It was one of the decisions she had made regarding this night, and now she second-guessed her choice of the evening's student hosts. Of her selection criteria, she had side-stepped the obvious, self-aggrandizing choices by which she would have picked the brightest and most articulate of students—kids who would dazzle and amaze unsuspecting parents as they entered the room, were handed the evening's agenda and shown to their areas of interest. Instead, she had asked Francis Danuta and Anne Marie Delucchi to host, pass out programs and direct traffic for extra credit. She had banked on Francis and Anne Marie assuming The Mantle of the Expert for the evening, and, as a result, their pride in scholarly engagement might gain traction. Oh, it was a gamble, alright, and, as the hour approached, she reconsidered her odds. That Francis would be well-meaning but awkward and operating at a loss all night was a sure thing; the boy was still growing into his skin. She hedged that with the largess and generosity she ascribed to the attending parents. Surely they would be—if amused by his shy confusion—polite, gentle and understanding. He might just come away from this evening feeling okay-to-good about his contribution. That which does not kill us...

Anne Marie was the long shot. The girl was off-color, erratically pruned and raised in the dark. Victoria had invited Anne Marie into this positive, productive role hoping her brief exposure to natural light might give her a glimpse at another side of herself—that she might feel useful, helpful, needed. That was her hope, though things could easily tip the other way with that girl, and Victoria would have to allocate a good portion of her attention to Anne Marie, at least for the first part of the evening.

"Hey, Ms. Merritt."

She turned to Francis in a tie. "Francis, hello, and you are right on time." She stepped aside, and he entered.

"Wow, it's different. I mean, it looks good, your room." He rapped on a desk.

"Thank you. We want the parents to see that we are organized, and that your time here is worthwhile. And, may I say you look quite professional tonight?"

"Yeah? Oh, this." He flipped his tie. "My mom, she said I should."

"It was a good choice."

"Like, what's all that?" He pointed to the back of the room.

"Those are goals agreed to by Pennsylvania's committee of education experts."

"Huh. Sorry, I—"

"Hey, look at this place." Anne Marie leaned in the doorway. "All dressed up and no place to go?"

Cleavage! Her waist-cinched, studded jean jacket flayed open, and, from beneath her green satin landslide of a neckline, there appeared the stereoscopic results of a full-effect Wonderbra. Tight, torn jeans and black, stiletto-heeled, ankle-top boots completed the presentation. Checking her watch, Victoria wondered if the buttons on that jacket were functional. No time for the girl to go home and change. "Welcome, Anne Marie."

"Damn." Francis whispered.

Anne Marie entered and clicked and blinged over to Victoria's desk. Her heels stopped followed by the diminishing tingles of thin metal bracelets. She took a quick visual tour. "Hmm, very nice. You've picked up."

Victoria shelved her reaction and showed her two students around the room, pointed out the labels at the heads of the rows, reviewed the programs stacked on a stool by the door and spoke briefly about the concepts taped up in back.

"Synthesize?" Francis asked.

Anne Marie rolled her eyes. "It's, like, *Depeche Mode*, you goof."

"Hmm. Yes, or, in this case, combining things to make something new. To intelligently put things together—and no one is a goof. Francis, please excuse us for a moment? Anne Marie, come with me, please?"

Victoria led down the hall a few doors. "We're going to the girls' room?" Anne Marie asked. The heels clicked, and the bracelets jingled past as Victoria held the door.

"It'll be just a moment," Victoria said. Inside, she invited Anne Marie to a sink.

"Huh?" Anne Marie asked.

"Here." Victoria stood behind Anne Marie and looked over the girl's shoulder into the mirror. "What do you see?"

Anne Marie pulled back and turned her head to answer. "Like, my English teacher? Behind me?"

"No, you, Anne Marie. What do you see when you see yourself, there in the mirror?"

"Can we go now? This is really weird."

"Please. Be honest."

"Okay." She shifted a hip and smiled original sin. "Like, I see one sexy bitch."

"I agree, Anne Marie. One attractive, fashionable and worldly woman."

"So, like what, then?"

Victoria moved from behind the girl and leaned back on a neighboring sink. Anne Marie faced her, arms crossed.

"The people attending our open house, the mothers, fathers, grandparents—your continental allure will be lost on them. They don't have the eye, the fashion awareness you've been born with. They'll likely find your cosmopolitan sense to be beyond their understanding, and things people don't understand, they easily dislike."

Anne Marie looked back to the mirror. "Then they can just kiss my—"

"Let's not waste your appeal on unaware people tonight. Why expend the energy? Let's save our special brand of sophistication for someone who can appreciate us." Victoria turned to her mirror and, with theatrical deliberation, buttoned the second-to-top button of her own blouse. She raised her chin for the top button. "Shall we button up until the last of our guests have gone home?"

Anne Marie stared at her for a cross-eyed moment, looked back to the mirror, turned and left.

The classroom was smaller with parents in it. They foraged about in large clothes touching things as if to assure themselves that education, the school and this teacher were real. They touched her desk as they passed: the doctor's wife, the mechanic, the claims adjuster. They ran their fingers down the long counter top along the dark windows. Victoria watched a mousy woman in a long colorless raincoat lift a corner of Victoria's desk planner from behind the bookshelves then drop it back into place as though she'd just seen a message from the devil. She turned to what had to be her husband, equally small in a grey work uniform and receding hair, and she whispered something to which his eyes darted nervously around the

room as though someone was listening. From behind her
desk, Victoria rang the tiny bell.

The grazing stopped, eyes front. "Would you please
find a seat? Anywhere? I have planned just a few minutes
of presentation followed by a Q&A before the bell to your
next class." The parents' seat selection process was
similar to their kids,' but slower.

Victoria stood behind her desk. "Thank you for coming
this evening. It is encouraging to see this turnout—such
parent involvement. I am Victoria Merritt. This is my first
year as a teacher, and I am thankful to have your kids as
my first students. They are interesting, funny, bright and
sometimes challenging. Their interpretation of our studies
is often unique. You may have met our two aides, Anne
Marie Delucchi and Francis Danuta. I am grateful for their
assistance."

Anne Marie grinned. Francis blushed.

She walked out from behind her desk. "Our
attainment goals for the year are posted in the back of the
room." Some of the parents turned in their seats. "You've
probably read through them by now. With those goals in
mind, your students are looking into the lives of some of
literature's oldest characters, heroes and heroines, family
struggles, conflicts over land, riches and power. I hope you
enjoy this brief PowerPoint presentation of our classes and
some of the stories we're reading."

"What's this? Parent school for dummies?!" he
laughed. His was a dark suit that nearly filled the open
door. He entered, sucked in his belly, buttoned his jacket
and, holding the button in place and his back to the wall,
side stepped down the first aisle. "Sorry we're late." He ran
a hand through thick black hair and looked back to the
empty doorway, "Rose!" His jowls shook.

On the other side of the room, Anne Marie scowled,
crossed her arms tightly and spun away toward the
windows.

"Rose, you comin?"

The door framed an average-sized woman in an understated suit, purse and heels. She smiled.

Victoria nodded and motioned, "Welcome. There are a few seats up here."

The woman looked to her husband.

"Okay, okay, just a minute. Christ." He shuffled back to the front, edged past Victoria and they sat—he with some effort on one cheek, sidesaddle.

The evening made an unscheduled stop as some of the men seated closest to him reconnected with their favorite barber. "Big Al" twisted awkwardly in his tiny seat to high fives and exchanged insider quips. Satisfied they were all still *Sixers* fans, the men settled in.

Victoria turned, tapped a key on her laptop and nodded to Francis at the light switches. Near dark, and, as their eyes adjusted, Herbie Hancock's *Maiden Voyage* awakened through the speakers. Images flashed tempo at the front of the room: blurred action shots of students entering, finding seats, Victoria addressing them, laughing, pointing, students' hands raised and then Shakespeare, Cate Blanchett, Hunt's painting of *The Pot of Basil*, Homer, George Clooney, Caligula, Claire Danes, Millais' painting of *Ophelia*, Delacroix's *The Death of Sardanapalus*, Judi Dench, Picasso's *Guernica* and the trailer for Ethan Hawke's *Hamlet 2000*. The images faded, the music trailed off and Francis hit the lights.

"What the hell was that?" Big Al asked. Parents rustled in their seats. Some stood and found safe distance along the windows.

"Well, I guess we're in the Q&A portion of the class." Victoria smiled and thought, maybe skip the PowerPoint next time. Or, end it earlier, before the severed head in *The Pot of Basil.*

The small nervous couple who had suspected the devil in the back of the room crept along the seams and were out the door like shadows.

"No, really. What *was* that?" Al asked. "I mean, like hell and damnation and our kids gotta see this? Like bloody heads and naked bodies?" Rippled murmurs in the aisles, pursed lips and furrowed brows topped unanimous body language.

Too much, too soon? They'll complain to the principal? Explain. "I hope what you take away from this evening is that your kids, our students, are enjoying themselves in our classes, that we share in lively critical discussions and that they are studying classic subjects—stories from the ancients to the middle ages, from Homer to Shakespeare."

"And, what's that got to do with the here and now and whatever the hell they're lookin at in the future? Sounds like a lot of handwringing over some old news, if you ask me." He looked like he'd been crammed into that seat for just about long enough and was struggling to extract himself without breaking something. His wife checked her watch. The bell rang for the next class, and parents started making their way out. He was on his feet. The desk fell away and clattered to rest as he cursed to himself and massaged a thigh.

"They are timeless stories of man's struggles from any age, from all ages. We hope to see—"

"Whatever." Al straightened and brushed his sleeves. "Just keep it G-rated, okay? I get word otherwise and you and me, we'll have words—you, me, and the principal. I cut his hair, known him for years. We gotta go now. Nice to meet ya."

He stopped by his wife at the door, turned, and pointed across the room, "Home by ten, Anne Marie!" His wife pulled at his sleeve. "It's still a goddam school night!"

December 2000: *Francis' Father*

Nick Danuta wasn't going to the open house. It was the end of the workday, and Nick Danuta leaned elbows on knees and felt the frozen earth course up through the plant locker room's steel bench and squeeze through his ass and into his guts. His head and wasted body sagged like wet canvas. Between his knees the pint bottle hung from his fingers, swayed and dropped. He nodded off to the memory:

They'd been kids. They pumped water from the well, weeded the garden and collected berries. They set snares for rabbits. He and little Helen chinked cracks under windows and around doors with newspaper and hung the laundry on the porch or near the smoky woodstove in winter. Raymond and he split wood. The three of them stacked it. None of that was hard for them. What was hard for the three Danuta kids was when they left their house, there in the woods every Monday, and climbed onto that yellow bus.

The worst part about the bus was Nuccio; he was always there in the back. Nuccio. The bastard got away with murder on those half-hour rides. He was years older than all the rest of them, and he just loved to dish out abuse to the little pukes. Raymond, Nick and Helen—that's how they lined up to wait for the bus each morning. Raymond, the biggest, the oldest, was first. Books under their arms, step up left, then right, keep your head down and try to find a seat near the front, away from Nuccio. Insults and stares is what they got. Almost never someone willing to slide over. Most times they just sat in the aisle, those kids—those wood-smoke-stinking kids from Skunk Hollow.

The boys' hair was parted and combed to one side, their shirts buttoned to the collar and tucked in their pants. Helen's skirt was proper length, hair brushed, pulled to a ponytail and tied with Mom's ribbons. Raymond wore the newest shoes. Long days at school, they each tried their best to keep invisible—eyes down, they drew themselves into overlooked spaces. They had lunch tickets but rarely used them. The attention they drew in the cafeteria line wasn't worth it. Stomachs knotted tight, they were skinny kids.

Helen and Raymond were the first to fall. Eight years of public school—the cruelty—got to be too much for Helen, and with her body changing over the summer, there was no way she was going back for ninth grade. She'd seen how it had gone for some of the other girls. Determined as Helen was—paid no attention to reasoning, cajoling, additional chores—Mom was that much more determined that Helen would begin ninth grade, chin up and on time. It was pure foolish to do battle with Mom. The summer bore down into August, and Helen went silent. Took to sucking her thumb. Everybody noticed, but no one said anything around Helen.

"Leave her alone," Raymond said. "It'll pass. She'll stop in her own time."

First day of school, they stood in a row at the intersection of dirt and pavement awaiting the bus: Raymond, Nick and Helen. Mom watched from up the county road; she probably thought she was out of sight. The bus doors opened. They filed aboard. Doors closed, and the bus pulled out.

It was as they knew it would be, on the bus again. No one offered a seat, someone shouted something about gagging and them sleeping with pigs. Nuccio was destroying a new kid's ball hat. Helen found a seat. The boys sat in the aisle near the front and bounced along in the heat.

A few miles up the road there came a choking smell of hot oil and burning rubber, and white smoke spewed in from the defroster and heater vents. It filled the bus, and kids screamed bloody murder. The driver pulled over, slammed on the brakes, threw the doors open and ordered everyone off. It was all shoving, and yelling and little ones being run asunder. The Danuta kids were first off. The driver directed them and the rest of the outpouring to stand in the new-mowed field at the rear. With most of the kids off, the driver made trips back into the smoke to extract the bruised and dazed younger ones. He did a head count.

"Everyone stay right where you are!" He ran back aboard the bus and grabbed the fire extinguisher. He pried the hood open, sprayed a fog into the smoking engine compartment, then stood back before sticking his head into the bay to check the damage. That was when Nuccio piped up.

"Oooo, scary! Like I'm shaking all over. I'll bet the little pukes are just peeing their pants."

Standing there in the back of the group, was Helen, her thumb in her mouth.

"Oh, looky over here at the stinky little thumb sucker."
He hooked her arm and yanked her to his side. "Let's see
if her diaper's wet."

Helen kept her head lowered and squirmed and
yanked as Nuccio grabbed her skirt and pulled it up to her
shoulders.

"Hey look, she really pissed her pants!"

Helen was in tears, her eyes slammed shut.

From somewhere in the crowd, Raymond leaped. He
landed like a hundred and forty pounds of bricks and
ripped Nuccio from Helen. Nuccio sprang back to his feet,
and Raymond hit him again and drove his head and
shoulders hard into the bastard's knees. They rolled
toward the bus. They clawed, and choked, and scratched
and punched. They kicked up sod, and no one could say
who was winning. They were under the bus. The kids
edged forward and stooped to see. From the dark beneath
the bus came a hollow, *thunk*. Quiet, then, but for solitary
heaving. The kids backed away as a bloody Nuccio crawled
into the light. The driver raced up to them just as Nick
landed screaming on his brother's foe. Legs clamped
around Nuccio's waist, Nick dug his thumbs deep into the
bastard's eyes. "Holy fuck!" The driver pried them apart.
He commanded them to sit. Nuccio collapsed crying,
blind, and helpless. "Jesus Christ!" The driver crawled
beneath the bus. It was some time that he lay under there
holding Raymond's still hand. Thirty-feet away she sat
and rocked in the grass humming, one shoe off, her skirt
hiked to her waist, and Helen sucked her thumb.

He'd put it behind him. Nick Danuta pulled steaming,
twelve-inch concrete blocks, two at a time, off wet steel
racks, and swung those blocks onto wooden pallets and
stacked those blocks chin high every day, all day, with one
break in the morning, lunch break at noon and one break
at three. It involved everything, stacking blocks: legs,
back, shoulders, neck, arms, hands and sphincter. No one
can do that bare-palmed, and Nick went through a pair of

leather, twenty-eight-dollar, Made in U.S.A. work gloves every three days. Small guys are fast, big guys are strong, but stacking fifty-pound blocks, they both need rhythm and momentum—rhythm, momentum and calories. Built like a spider, belt cinched high, he ate every chance he got. They all did, those guys working at the plant. They just worked, and sweat and ate. Break time, they ate. Noon whistle blew and everything shut down but the third-story mixer, they ate. Summers, they sat on the dirt in a circle in the shade of one of those forklifts and ate from hinged lunch boxes and brown paper bags. One drank coffee from a thermos, and the rest bought Pepsi from the machine, and it was a bad day if the machine was empty. Made for a bad afternoon.

Holiday shut down, the plant was quiet and Nick Danuta sat on a narrow steel bench in the thick cement dust of the dark locker room. His hands ached; they always ached. His back, too—always his back. Was it the suffocating summers that were the worst or this damned winter? Bone-to-bone he leaned his elbows to his knees, his shoulders stuttered and he coughed deep, wet coughs.

As they left the yard today, one of the guys yelled, "Say hi to the wife and kids!" The bastard.

Wife, huh. You couldn't say what he had was a wife, or a family, but the woman still slept in the same house, fed the kids, got them off to school. Keeping up the front for her damned church. Glimpses he got of her in the daylight hours, she was still what would be called an attractive woman; a little heavier than their first few years together, she worked cosmetics at that fat-ass department store and paid the bills on time. She just turned from him one day forever, back there awhile and continued with her life; separate lives in separate rooms from then on. Those kids. Probably what ruined their marriage. Parasites. He had to use some heavy shit to keep them in line: the son, the daughter—the wife. Had to get verbal, and—you life-sucking bastards—physical. They cowered around him, though Francis had shot up recently and was starting to fill out and may soon show some color. The fucking kid was hard to read, too quiet. Moody. The kid would probably just go off one day. That wouldn't be good. He'd likely kill the boy—kill the boy and set fire to the whole damned mess.

He wouldn't go home just yet, as he didn't every night. He'd go directly to the bar across the swamp, drink to failure and wake up at the house in a heap somewhere in the vicinity of his cot in the pantry. Damn bottle was empty.

January 2001: *William Howard Hill, M.Ed., Principal*

William Howard Hill, Principal, ran the school on a clock and a bell. Howie, as the teachers called him, stood 5'6" on inserts, if no one was measuring. He was all U.S. Issue with receding hair clipped short at the sides the way he and Big Al liked it and slicked-on Pro Gel to keep the remaining top wisps in place. His jutting chin and piranha under bite bespoke power and all business; his people were in line, and, "Did you really expect to just break ranks, there, young lady?" He didn't walk, tromping about like some aimless student. No, his brown spit-shines glided just a quarter inch above the decks. Order and quiet, not an echo between classes down those polished and ever-lockered halls. He was posture perfect, his chest arriving first; it was a genetic thing, his chest—a bandy rooster's like his father's. Making the early hour, pre-start rounds, that first day back from the Christmas holidays, he stopped at the little office by the cafeteria and checked in on the school counselor. "You have this, Marge, this morning's meeting?"

She nodded.

He moved on to the faculty lounge. He cracked the door and peeked in. The butch-cut sage of the English

department threw an empty paper cup at the door,
"Persona non-grata, Howie. Get thee gone." Howie smiled,
winked and closed the door. Moving on to the gym, the
jocks were spotting each other pumping iron. One yelled,
"Hey Mr. Hill, nice pecs!" Howie laughed and waved,
absorbing their admiration. Checking his tie in the trophy
case, he moved to his next checkpoint. Ever smooth,
William Howard Hill.

Victoria formed a pretty clear picture of the narrow
church-and-pie balance of his world during her first job
interview. Twenty minutes into it, things were going well—
formally but well—when the principled man in the brown
suit asked, "And, you're a Jewess?" The question hung on
her uncloven stare.

Back in his office, half-an-hour before the students
would be buzzed in for the start of the second semester,
Howie pressed the red button on his phone. "Attention.
Faculty. Please. May I have your attention? All teachers
please report to the auditorium immediately. All teachers.
Come to the auditorium immediately. Now people!"

"Front rows, please. Everyone down front, each seat,
fill them in, please, each seat, now. Don, move over one."
Howie directed from somewhere at the front of the
auditorium obscured by the entering faculty. Once they
were seated, he paced along the knees of the front row,
hands behind his back.

"We have a delicate situation folks—something of
which some of you may be aware, and I'll turn it over to
Marge, now. Marge?"

Tall and business-like in suit and heels, Marge
Sweeney clicked briskly down the aisle from the back of
the theater and took her post, front dead center. They
liked Marge. The kids did, too. Smart, efficient,
empathetic, champion of the disenfranchised—mid-forties
and laugh lines sticking out the sides of little designer
glasses and wrapping nearly around her cropped blond
head. She spent most of her time with students or on the

phone to county agencies in her small counseling office just off the cafeteria. Seeing her in the teachers' lounge, or passing her in the hallway, her lipstick, fresh but cursory—a bit crooked—she frequently looked like she'd just been crying.

"Hi guys, welcome back and I'll be brief. As Howie said, by now some of you are aware that we had a tragedy over the holidays—a couple, actually. As far as our school, they most directly impact the senior class. First-of-all, Donald Mahonski succumbed to leukemia over Christmas. You may not have known Donald. He was quiet, small—just a pup. Howie has sent condolences to the family on our behalf, and there's a poster and collection container for the family in the cafeteria and one in the office. The Mahonski's never had much. Now they have less. Please pitch in. Thanks, Howie.

Now, something requiring our immediate and on-going, attention: The Danuta kids—Francis and Kathy—lost their dad. Christmas Eve, Nicholas Danuta committed suicide."

Teachers murmured, twisted and stretched around to the row behind and whispered out across and beyond those next to them.

"Kathy, Francis and their mother's—Isabel's—home life has always been challenging—tragic—but this takes it much further. The kids are getting professional counseling, and I'm asking all of us to give them a little leeway and to be especially vigilant and sensitive to student interactions for these next few months. We shouldn't coddle them, please. It's tough, but we have to be neutral—sensitive, aware and neutral. These kids don't need more focus than they're already getting. If you have any questions, or would like to discuss this with greater detail, please come see me, and we'll spend as long as we need. Howie?"

Victoria's consciousness nearly left. Black holes in her vision, acid throat, and her heart thumped in her head. She gripped both sweating armrests, lifted herself from her seat and followed the murmuring teachers from the auditorium.

She had a few minutes before her students would arrive. Unsteady, she stepped out to the loading dock. In freezing wind and ice puddles, she trembled the lighter, the cigarette—that awful summer at home, the church, her father. A flock of silver and white circled against a low, heavy sky. The birds flipped, dove and banked as one, and were gone in an instant.

"You okay?" The custodian came around the side of a truck parked below and, gloved hands on the edge of the dock, hoisted himself up like out of a pool. "Bad night's sleep? You really gotta get a good eight hours."

She took a drag and sent it into the wind with whatever it was she was about to say.

"You want to come into the receiving shack? Warmer in there."

"No, thank you. I just needed a break." She hugged her arms tightly around her. "We just heard some bad news, sad news." Bundled in down and ballooned out like The Michelin Man, he was younger than she first thought, now that she actually looked at him. Taller. His eyes.

"The Danuta kids?"

"Yes."

"Sorry to say, but no great loss. Their old man was a real piece of work—mean drunk. You see that girl, the bruises—the daughter? Suicide's not enough for some pricks. He shoulda done it years ago—save everybody a lot of grief. Want me to watch your class while you take five?"

"I— No, I'll be fine in a moment."

He came over, pulled off a glove and presented a thick ivory hand. "I'm Max, I clean your room every night."

His hand was warm, solid. "Victoria Merritt."

"I knew we'd get around to it, you and me—meeting. Sorry it's like this. If you need anything, like, I don't know, just ask. Okay? Extra towels, room rearranged, light bulbs, whatever."

"Thank you."

How It Went Down Over Christmas Break

December 24, 2000: *Francis Danuta's Mother*

Isabel Danuta smiled into the front room mirror, adjusted her collar and stepped out to catch the 11:27 bus to Bateman's Fashions. Flurries in the air, downtown was at its best blanketed with snow for the holidays; it really brought out the shoppers. The snow, the lights, the music piped through the streets. Miele's Gifts would be packed, the Miele sisters all abuzz assisting customers looking for unique stocking stuffers, and you couldn't walk down Pine Street without bumping into half a dozen people you knew. The bus had been dropping her off in front of the bank, just half a block from Bateman's, for the past fifteen years; she was on her third driver. He was from North Carolina with one wife, one mother-in-law, three kids and fourteen grandchildren. For the past eight years, she'd looked forward to her twenty-minute ride to work, taking the front side seat by the door over the wheel well. From there, he and she could chat. Well, mostly he, sharing installments of his life from, "Back in Norf Cackalacky," and his rolling commentary on the day's news, and, "I'll tell you what. If I was coachin them *Eagles*, they'd be some changes made, darlin. Big changes! Watch yer step, dear. See ya in the mornin light."

"Thank you, Walter, see you in the morning light." She stepped onto the curb and felt the sole of her boot find its grip in the snow. The bus heat sucked away as the doors closed, and, in the swirling wake, she waited for the blinking, *WALK*.

The town center's window displays were magic, each store outdoing its neighbor. Snowy drifts, sleighs, suspended stars, ornaments, animated elves and reindeer and miniature railroads—all lit magically and accompanied by the celestial ringing of Salvation Army bells from every other corner. Few shoppers had change left in their pockets this time of year. She entered through the front door and waved to part-time Irene. She passed around the cosmetics counter, headed upstairs through intimate apparel and back to the storeroom and staff area. She put her purse and gloves in her locker, hung her coat and scarf on the employees' rack, pulled off her boots and placed them near the heater vent to dry. There were a couple women from hosiery ahead of her at the time clock chattering about how they were going to spend their extra pay from these ten-hour holiday shifts. Hers always went straight to Frankie and Kathy. Up next, she punched in.

December 24, 2000: *Francis Danuta's Father*

At the concrete block plant, Nick Danuta punched out. His hands ached; they always ached. His back, too. Always his back. Was it the suffocating summers that were the worst or this damned blue steel winter? Bone-to-bone he leaned his elbows to his knees, his head in his hands, his shoulders jacked like tent poles, and he coughed. Half day, start of the holiday plant shut down. A week off and he had his bonus check. The bar would cash it.

December 24, 2000: *Francis Danuta's Sister*

Kathy Danuta rose late to an empty house. Mom would be at work, and Frankie was off to join his nerd friends in their every-waking-moment *Total Combat* marathon. Coming downstairs way after noon, she loved the smell of the tree in the corner. Frankie had dragged it in, put it up and filled the water. Today, she'd be stringing lights and dressing it up like Macy's from head to toe. She bare-footed across the front room's new cold linoleum and avoided the patch of exposed subfloor going into the kitchen. Splinters. The kitchen was next on the list for improvements which would probably be in another ten years. Chai tea and a one-cup measure of Honey Nut Cheerios and almond milk. She was sixteen, trim and pretty and intended to keep it that way. Enjoying her brunch, she ordered the day:

- *Call Darryl, and thank him for walking her home last night*
- *Tell him she was baking cookies today and she would drop off a box*
- *Mention that she and Shawn were going up to the sled hill Friday night at seven*
- *Bake the cookies*
- *Clean up the mess because Frankie was such a weird clean-freak*
- *Find the ladder, and get the tree decorations out of the attic*
- *Trim the tree*
- *Read awhile*
- *Take a shower*
- *Go to the sub shop and hang out*

An hour after calling Darryl—she left a message—the house, and half a block in each direction, smelled of vanilla, cinnamon and sugar. Dozens of cookies sparkled and cooled on racks. Now, for the Christmas boxes. She found the wooden step ladder languishing against their slumped garage in the alley, banged it on her shin getting it through the kitchen, hauled it upstairs, climbed into the dark, freezing, spider-webs-all-over-the-place attic and retrieved the decorations. Enough to defeat a lesser soul. Boxes stacked, hands frozen, she closed the attic and stashed the ladder by the back door. She stopped to twist the thermostat, put on a Christmas CD and bellowed, "Tree, stand aware! This shall ever be known as the Great and Incomparable Kathy Danuta Plain-Jane-Spruce-Tree Transformation." And, it was. A hundred twinkling lights buried deep in its boughs, it proudly presented glass ornaments from her mother's childhood, handmade, wrinkled paper snowflakes and reindeer from Frankie's and her elementary years and colorful and exotic mementos from Nana's travels.

"Phew." She stepped back. "You did it again, Kathy, such an artist. Would you share your inspiration with our audience? Oh, I'd love to, but I really need a nap. Let me just say that I couldn't have done it without the rest of the team. I know our defense had a few issues today, but I picked up the slack and turned things around for a win."

She put the empty boxes out by the ladder, came back in, bolted the door and cuddled in the afghan on the couch with her book and Bing Crosby.

She woke to a thump in the dark. There, again, as she sat up. Quiet, now, and the tree was shimmering. Beautiful.

Crash! A fist punctured the door glass, reached in and unbolted the lock. Her dad fell into the room.

She screamed, shot up and ran to the kitchen. He rose from the shattered glass on rubber legs, wiped his mouth on his sleeve and vomited into the center of the floor splashing everything within three feet.

"Oh my God! Fuck you! Get out! Get the fuck out of here you fucking monster!" She searched around and grabbed a pot.

"Yeah? Well, fuck you back."

He lurched toward her, veered sideways and into the tree. He straddled branches as it listed and sank to the floor.

Kathy rushed into the room. "You asshole, I hate you!" She slipped in the puke, dropped to her butt and slid feet first into him. She sprang up, dug both hands into his scalp and pulled him out of the tree by his hair. On his feet, again, he turned, unleashed a crushing backhand and sent her flying. She slammed onto the stairs, an unconscious heap.

"Little bastards think they own the place, do they? Do they? Eh?" Unsteady, he headed for the back door and out to the garage. He burst through the rotted side door and fell into the dark workbench. Feeling for the drawer, "Own the place, eh? Own my ass...uh-huh..."

He was running out of steam. He returned through the kitchen to the front room. Both hands, he raised the .44 to the stairs at the upside-down tangle of inert flesh and hair that was Kathy. Bloody shards poked from his knuckles. The room tilted.

December 24, 2000: *Francis Danuta*

Francis Danuta made the call. He spoke to his mom's brother, the deputy. "Uncle Bobby, Dad's dead."

By the time the deputies and the coroner arrived, the washer was running, and the place smelled like Lysol. Kathy shook, swollen eyes, bloody and bruised. She was wrapped tight in the afghan. A young woman, a paramedic, kneeled beside her and whispered while applying butterfly bandages to her nose, eyebrow and the edges of her mouth. Her partner finished with the IV and went out for the stretcher.

Francis was white, his voice unsteady, and his fingers crawled like they were trying to leave the house. The deputy, his uncle, came back into the front room. He carried the gun in a plastic bag, dropped it on a side table and asked Francis, "Were you here? When it happened?"

"Yeah, I was here."

"He did this to Kathy while you were here?"

"No, no. I came home after that. I thought she was dead—that Kathy was dead."

"So, Kathy was unconscious when you got home?"

"Yeah, she wasn't moving. All bloody—like there." He pointed to the stairs.

"No one else was here?"

"No."

"Then what?"

"What, what?"

"What'd you do?"

"I called you. I called the sheriff."

"After you heard the shot?"

Francis' eyes rolled around the room and stopped back at Kathy as her attendants strapped her to the stretcher. "Yeah."

"Then you called."

"Yeah."

"Right after you heard the shot?"

"Yeah, I—"

"Right after? Immediately after?"

"Yeah, I guess. Like, almost."

"You knew the bastard was dead, then you called. Like you went in and checked his pulse?"

"No, I—"

"Then you thought it would be a good time to do some house cleaning, maybe do the laundry? Or did you do some of that before you called me?"

"Uncle Bobby, can we clean up the pantry? Get the cot out of there before Mom knows? It's too awful, and we gotta fix that window. We gotta put the tree back up and somebody's gotta fix that window, like, with the cold blowing in, and all. Somebody broke that window."

The coroner came in from the kitchen. "We're done, here, Robert. You got my vote and it's your call." He patted Francis on the shoulder, stepped out and closed the door behind him. He called back in through the broken glass, "Poker Friday?"

"Right," the deputy said. He peeled blue gloves and turned to Francis, "Okay, Frankie. You asked for it. You've got twenty minutes to clean that bastard's shit off the wall, but I'm not helping. I'll be out front in the car; twenty minutes, Frankie, then, I tell sis."

January 2001: *Second Semester and Back from the Break*

The students rolled into Victoria's room in twos and threes, arms over each other's shoulders, fist bumped, knocked desks aside and caught up on holiday adventures. It was like starting over, only worse. They were wet. The cold of the loading dock stuck to her.

She stood, clipboard roster folded into her arms, and glanced at the clock above the door. It resembled the timer on her stove: mute, mechanical, detached.

The painful sounds of thirty-one teens in motion receded.

Time, she thought: small, minute jerks of a gray needle on a white dial, ever forward. To what end? We propose to know where it's been, but can only guess where it's going or if it will stop. So much we wish away; here demonstrated by thawing students back from the holidays smelling of wet wool, cigarettes and toothpaste, and they can't wait until this period is over, and better yet, lunch and, best of all, Friday night—and then the next, and the next until summer. Huh. Look at that. Only five minutes and they're seated. Quiet. Francis Danuta is missing.

"First, welcome back to your favorite class and, by far and away, your favorite teacher."

"Boooo!" They laughed.

"With all sincerity, I welcome you back. I do enjoy you, your gaiety and wit, and I am confident that with just a bit more of my nudging most of you will leave here competently literate by the end of the semester.

Before we begin, I would like us to remember Donald Mahonski. You have heard that Donald's fight with leukemia has ended. Can we dedicate a moment of silence, please, in remembrance and respect?"

"Anne Marie, will you please recall for the class what we studied before the holidays? Anne? Anne Marie?"

Anne Marie spun and faced front. "Sorry, had to remind Monica not to talk in class."

"We thank you. Would you please refresh our memories on what we were studying last semester, before the break?"

"Guinevere."

"Hmm, yes, Guinevere was a major player. And, what do you recall about Guinevere?"

"Like you said, she was a 'major player'—if ya get what I'm saying."

"Okay, alright. Class, please? Thank-you, Anne. Well said. You will recall that we examined heroes as portrayed in literature, Arthur being one." Turning to the whiteboard she wrote a squeaking black column of numbers. Will someone tell me the characteristics describing our tragic Greek heroes? Just call them out."

"Orphans against tyrants!"

"Weird birth!"

"Exile, searching, battles!"

"Returns and saves the family, *Ta-daah!*"

The marker squealed, its solvent overpowering the cigarettes and wet wool. She placed the pen in the tray, turned to the class and smiled. "Thank you."

Just like that, they were back and into their rhythm—her rhythm. They were back to the reading, the writing, the animated if sometimes free-wheeling class discussions, her repetitious grammar and punctuation drumming and her—If I have to repeat this one more time I think I will just lie down here behind this desk, fold my arms over my bosom and give up the ghost—thoughts.

A new student had joined the class, a transfer junior with a sealed file from a private school and something familiar about her. She wasn't one quick to warm to strangers, so Victoria didn't press it. Okay, have it your way, she thought. We'll just give it some time.

If one of the boys was within five feet of the new girl with that thick as your wrist, tight and perfect ebony braid reaching three inches below her waist and finally lighting on her short, fit, wool skirt—the girl with the carved cheekbones, darkly accented green eyes and full and clear-glossed lips—well, that was scented bath water he smelled, and it made him a little dizzy. Where Anne Marie was a wonderfully precocious girl, Faye Sunami was a woman. Faye didn't laugh or smile, and her glance never traveled more than three feet from her face. Head held high, she moved with the erect control of a ballerina, and most boys couldn't follow her between classes for more than a few precious seconds before breaking into a sweat and adjusting the change in their pockets. Within a week of her arrival, the two Hazzard brothers, Bomber and Rusty, and Maynard Burton, two-time state wrestling champ and part-time delinquent, found where she lived up Sulphur Springs Road, and that her dad, a dark, limping hairy cuss with tattoos up the side of his face and a holstered ax on his belt, had a huge and honest-to-God live pacing African lion on a rattling chain in a concrete pen with an iron gate alongside their two-story, rundown dump of a house. This was seen with their very own eyes from up close and with great cunning.

Two weeks into the new semester, Francis Danuta returned to school. He felt naked. They were all staring, watching, waiting for something from him. His stomach cramped as he walked. He hadn't eaten this morning; he couldn't. They all knew what had happened over Christmas, and now they stared and, like, what, expected him to split in half, or something? Blushing, he sat, kept his head down and tried to look busy. He opened a book and mechanically copied its text onto his yellow tablet until Ms. Merritt gained the class's attention. Behind him, there was a new girl. He heard her slide a book across her desk, open it, sigh and click her pen, *read-y*. It seemed just an instant later the class was on its feet and out the door. He was slow to awaken, book still open, his hand asleep on the yellow tablet. Just the two of them remaining, Victoria asked, "Francis?"

January 2001: *The Part About Victoria's Father*

Late afternoon, Marge and Victoria sat at a corner table and had the hotel bar to themselves. "Your class and P.E. are the only two classes Francis and Donald had in common, Victoria. It's your class that's taken the holiday's impact. Coach probably isn't aware, in his own little gym world. He didn't attend Howie's meeting." Marge smiled. "He's probably still marking Donald absent; licking his chops over assigning extra laps and push-ups when he returns."

Marge had impressed Victoria those first few months of school: her pace, the passion she poured into counseling the kids, wearing her emotions openly. Genuine.

"I visited Donald's family a few times those last days—quiet, solid people, Jehovah's Witnesses," Marge said. "We sat in their tiny living room on second hand furniture and prayed, for what good it did. I always felt foolish, overdressed. They have a peace about them, as little as they have or want. I guess that's at the center of it, the not wanting. You have to know that every cent from our collection went right to Kingdom Hall. Deluded or not, and who's to say, those people are committed.

So, shall we talk about why you asked me here, bought me a drink?"

"Yes, but if you'll excuse me for just a moment?" Victoria slid from her chair and headed to the ladies' room. She had invited Marge to the grand old hotel on the other side of the river, a place rarely frequented by anyone they knew. Coach and his cronies would be at the Southern Grill by now for their brewed rehash of Friday's game. The women of the faculty who had a taste for an occasional glass would be hanging their coats just inside the door at the motel steakhouse up the pike.

In the ladies' room, Victoria leaned on the long white marble counter top and took a deep breath. She stepped away and echoed past herself in seven gilt-framed mirrors to the far end and back. The architecture was a solid, grounding distraction, the quality and scale from a long-gone era. Heavy porcelain, inlaid tiles and the ornate brass fixtures: nouveau sconces, towel holders, soap dishes, door latches and hinges. Harry Houdini slept here. She was back at the first mirror.

When did she become this adult? She touched her cheek. It had been nearly twenty years since her Dad. No one knew, no one guessed when they saw her. They thought she was able, that her life was easy. That hurt little girl who was she—still here, in this mirror, hidden by this face, this high school teacher, this big alone person.

She stalled in the luxurious restroom in the grand hotel, and did she really want to tell her story to Marge? Maybe just say she empathized with Francis and wanted to help him. Maybe just ask Marge's advice. Or, don't bring it up at all. She washed her hands, tossed the towel into the corner wicker and headed out.

"Another glass, ladies?" the bartender asked.

"Victoria?" Marge asked.

"Yes, thank you."

"Be right back." He winked.

"Did he wink?" Marge asked.

"I don't think so. I don't know. I miss these things."

"I think he winked. He definitely winked. Nice butt."

"Marge? When you told us about the Danuta kids—Francis and Kathy—it took my breath."

"It's awful, isn't it? Poor kids, and Isabel? Dear Isabel, on her treadmill, trying to keep house and family going. For years, she put up with that—that man. Then this. Suicide's the big 'fuck you,' but I don't think it was that with him. Probably an accident. I visited them a couple times, the kids' bruises and all. It was pretty obvious where they came from, but hard to prove. The father didn't talk; no emotion. Just sat there in the corner like a bag of rocks."

"They're never going to be able to put it behind them; those kids will be dragging this weight all their lives," Victoria said.

"We're doing what we can. Counseling."

"It won't help. Therapy will just give the kids a few tools to mask their pain. They will never be rid of it. And, if they ever actually were—rid of it—well, wouldn't that be a sickness in itself?"

Marge turned her chair full on, crossed her legs and extended long hands over the ends of the armrests, "Victoria?"

The bartender returned with their drinks and started to say something. Marge waved him away.

Victoria began: "Our family was somewhat like Donald's, poor, religious. Ours was a small town in Dutch country; Catawissa. Quiet and not a care. There's a green park along the river, slow, narrow streets winding with the creek. It was like another century. Gardening, canning, picnics." She took a sip. "Mom at home, Dad full time at the carpet mill, part time church custodian. The church unadorned; Dad kept it spotless. Everything in its place,

everyone in their place and married: Dad, Mom, her
brothers and their families—except for her youngest
brother, Uncle Richard, a bachelor."

"A rare experience, being raised on such a postcard,"
Marge said.

Victoria lowered her glass and folded her hands. "We
kids were just kids, all lumped together regardless of our
ages: neighbors, brothers, sisters, cousins, preteens and
preschoolers playing hide-and-seek and kickball in the
park at the edge of town. The only distinction between us
was Congregational or Methodist, and, well, that wasn't a
lot. Sometimes Uncle Richard would show up on his
bicycle waving his scarf and cheer us as we rounded the
bases."

"He worked at the mill, too?"

"Richard worked in the design department, a gifted
artist. He was a bit of an embarrassment to mom, his
fashion awareness and always commenting on her shoes,
her perfume. She and Dad argued about Richard. We kids
loved him. He cried out loud when Dad died."

"When was that?"

"I was six. Mom had pulled the chicken out of the oven
and set it on top of the stove and Dad was late for supper.
She sent me over to the church to get him. I pushed the
screen door open a crack and went into the dark, just a
few steps; it smelled clean and silent, the empty church. I
had never been inside with no one there. I called for him,
quiet, a whisper. Then, again, louder. I couldn't see. My
eyes adjusted, and I did."

She slid the napkin from beneath her glass, folded it
twice and covered it with her hand. Her voice went flat.
"His shoe and hat, on the floor. He hung from a rope in
the rafters, my dad. I couldn't breathe. I ran for mom."

"Victoria, I'm sorry." She waved two fingers toward the
bartender, reached over and placed her hand on
Victoria's.

"We moved away shortly after that. I went back a little
over a year ago, before grad school. Nothing's changed,

except we're not there and Richard's in New York."

"How was your mother, I mean, how did she cope? How were you? How did she help you through this? You were six."

"She is a survivor, practical. Her warmth cooled to duty, efficiency. I must allow her that. She was in shock, we all were. She moved us away and in with her great aunt in Harrisburg and never looked back. I needed her more than ever. I lost them both."

"She had a lot to deal with, but you should have come first."

"Each night, when I closed my eyes, I saw his hat—my dad's hat."

"Do you still?

"Sometimes. Sometimes I wake to it. And sometimes Mom's hands, her red fists—when I told her, when I ran and told her. She backed up against the sink, pounded her fists on it, then was out the door. I waited, alone, in the kitchen, at the table. Two of my aunts came over. We watched the news and *Happy Days*."

Marge stood, edged around and laid her hands on Victoria's shoulders. She squeezed.

Victoria relaxed, some. She addressed her lap, "Dad's father came out of the woodwork and tried to fill in once-in-a-while, more as I got older—as he got older." She twisted up and looked at Marge. "I spent summers at Pop's cabin not far from here. Looking back, I think Pop felt responsible—responsible for our bad luck, his son. So, he did the things he wished his son had stuck around to do: took me fishing, pointed out deer tracks along the streams, bought me popsicles at the ball games and he could draw."

Marge tapped Victoria's shoulders. She went around the table and eased into her chair.

"He drew anything I'd ask at the kitchen table after supper. I watched those scrubbed hands still showing remains of the cars he had worked on that day. He penciled airplanes, cars, birds and rabbits from his imagination. Friday nights, we watched boxing on his little TV."

"And, your mother, what explanation? About your father?"

Victoria pushed the folded napkin to the center of the table. "She said my father was troubled."

"That's it?"

"That's all she offered, and I guess she thought it was all I needed. I needed more. Right then I needed someone to tell me I wasn't his trouble, that he loved me, that she loved me, that I wasn't my father's trouble."

"It wasn't you."

"I know. I've put it together over the years. My dad and mom's brother—Richard—and mom finding them. It's been a lot to deal with. But the family has it buried, like nothing happened. 'Dad was troubled.' Mom has a new guy with her in Harrisburg, a good guy. Back in Dutch country, new kids play at the park, there are concerts, picnic reunions and everything is back to slow and normal in Catawissa."

"You've seen someone professional, talked this through?"

Victoria laced her fingers together on the table. "As the years passed, I've self-adjusted."

"You're sure about that?"

"Marge, the Danutas—Francis."

"Yes?"

"I want to help him, if I can, maybe as a friend. He's drifting. He's a sweet kid who's going to blow away from us in the next storm."

"What would you do?"

"I'm not sure. Help me here. I'd adopt him if I could. I care, and I'd like him to know that, without pushing him."

"Victoria, is this for you or him?"

Victoria lowered her eyes.

February 2001: *The First Part About Francis and Faye*

It took just a month until a plump, school-wide resentment for the new girl ripened. The boys were intimidated by Faye's beauty, her presence, her distanced self-confidence, and they handled that as clumsily as everything else they didn't understand and couldn't control: with a lot of locker room crowing and chest thumping. But, they had plenty to keep them busy with the other girls and sports and cars and hunting and keggers, so who cared if the little foreign freak noticed them or not, right? However, a pack of girls, and Anne Marie in particular, really had their hackles up.

It was white noise to Francis: the girls, the lectures, the locker room—it floated there on his pain. It wasn't huge, the pain, just unshakeable, about an inch-and-a-half behind his eyes. Ranging between a one and a ten, it was a dull three most of the time and it was twenty-four-

seven. He'd done what he had to do, and now he had to
stick to it: to remember what he said to the sheriff the last
time and every time they asked the same questions, again
and again. He continued coming to class in a fog, drifting
between numbing Christmas nightmares, his body going
cold and hot without notice, weird cramps—Like, toe
cramps?—and a curious twinge whenever the new girl was
near. He waffled back and forth from wishing he was still
in the dark-and-nothing-void before he was born, to
leaving all of this and escaping with her into her light and
the foreign air she breathed and to wherever it was she
came from.

*

From out in the hallway, Anne Marie watched the new
girl place her books on her desk and slide into her seat.
Anne Marie waited until the class—her audience—was
seated. She entered the classroom, passed down Francis'
row, aimed an articulate hip at the new girl's books, pens
and tablets and sent them flying into the aisle. It was a
perfect hit. The class watched in silence as Francis
jumped up crimson, edged around his desk and, for the
next twenty seconds, knelt and raised, knelt and raised
and picked up the clutter and replaced the books and
pens and tablets semi-ordered onto Faye's desk. Faye sat
unblinking, her focus forward, hands-in-her-lap. Francis
took his seat.

"Thank you, Francis," Victoria said.

1983: *The Part About Victoria and Her Mother*

Shortly after Victoria's father's death, her mother moved them to Harrisburg—in with her mother's Great Aunt Hannah and Uncle Bill, poor people who, years ago, had their dreams beaten out of them. They lived in a weathered and dried up two-story. The house was nearly unfurnished. Aunt Hannah worked nights cleaning a few nearby offices and Uncle Bill, an ailing retired coal miner, sat in a corner watching reruns of *The Rockford Files* and coughing into a Folgers can. This was interrupted by trips to the fridge for a Pabst and trips to the john to "bleed the Pabst."

"Grace, Bill's color isn't good." That's what Victoria heard Aunt Hannah tell her mom. Playing on the floor with her farm set the next day, Victoria looked more closely at Uncle Bill and thought, kinda purple. Also, she heard her mother on the phone telling someone that she was dead inside and that, "This place makes my skin crawl." Victoria hoped they wouldn't be staying with Aunt Hannah and Uncle Bill much longer.

In a few weeks, and thanks to one of Bill's old mining buddies, Grace was hired as an entry-level administrative assistant in the state's Department of Environmental Resources. A month later, they moved out.

They were led up a narrow stairway with a thick wool runner to a hardwood landing and let into what was to become their new home. The dark oak floors and moldings shined, the walls were freshly painted, the brass switch plates and the curtain sheers at the large bay window overlooking the street glowed in the afternoon sun. And, the piano.

"Mom, a piano!" Gleaming, deep-lacquered black and without a scratch, it was a Yamaha studio model with a matching bench.

"Just been tuned, too," the landlord said. "Mother played."

He showed them through the bright kitchen, past a huge claw-foot tub in the spacious bath and into two bedrooms at the rear of the apartment, each with a window looking out across a cobbled parking lot to the elementary school playground.

"And, you're just two blocks from your office, Ms. Merritt."

"We'll take it."

That first week was a parade of boxes and deliverymen up and down their stairs, Grace and Victoria arranging things just so, catching the bus out front to the grocery store and exploring their new neighborhood in the early evenings on foot. They toured the new school, liked what they saw, and Victoria was enrolled in the second grade and an after-school arts program. Things were set.

A month later, Grace's skin still crawled. She was fine hustling Victoria to school, herself to work, shuffling papers from one office to the next, racing back to the school, fixing supper, baths and to bed; but that's when it wouldn't stop. When the lights were out and the apartment was quiet, her skin just kept going. Weekends, she couldn't breathe, couldn't relax. They'd walk to the park, go to a movie, stop in to the pet shop, the library, fast food—all the fun and easy things, and they made her crazy. She wasn't sleeping, her stomach churned, and she might need help—something, someone to lean on. Jesus.

A far cry from the little Christ Church of Catawissa, the First Trinity Episcopal was a buttressed baroque castle. Its spire and bell tower, topped by what appeared to be the handle of a sword, were taken into serious consideration by air traffic control. As they entered, Grace and Victoria's wind was squeezed from them and sent into the heights of the sanctuary where stained glass on all sides alternated between demons and saints, lambs and executions. This was a Jesus you didn't just take to a ballgame. The organ shook their lungs as Bach's *Fantasia in G Minor* was wrapping up, and Grace noted the organist was quite good. The pews were nearly full. They found a couple open spaces up front, and the rafters echoed to silence. Amidst congregational coughing and people settling in, a velvet-robed, rotund and pasty priest stepped into the pulpit far above them. Short fat fingers tapped the mic, and their necks were going to be sore from this.

"Welcome travelers to the house of God and the love of his son Jesus Christ. In him all things are made whole. Before we begin this morning's service, there are a few housekeeping items I'd like to share. First, the casserole supper hosted by The Jolly Workers class has been moved from next Saturday at seven to Friday at six."

"Saturday at six!" the organist loudly whispered.

Covering his mic, he looked left. "Huh?"

"It's still Saturday. Saturday at six."

Back to the mic. "Excuse me, it's Saturday at six."

"And, there will be auditions for the new adult choir this Wednesday at eight, and I encourage anyone who has been hiding their talents under a bushel to show up and raise your voice in praise. By the way, we have new gowns for the choir this year—purple. Maybe you'd call it magenta, with red trim, crimson, a bright crimson actually—more of an orange in the right light, and I think they look pretty great, myself."

"Seven," whispered the organist.

"What, NOW, Gladys?!" He boomed into the mic.

"Choir at seven." She held up her fingers.

He was flushed and sweating. "I stand corrected. Choir's at seven, and I don't know where I got these notes." He fussed his hands through his robe. "Probably left the final draft in my wedding robe. Which does remind me that the flowers today are from yesterday's wedding, the marriage of Daniel Fitzgerald and Sandra Fitzpatrick." He grinned baby corn teeth. "It would be easy to make a joke about that, kind of a word play, you know? Fitzgerald, Fitzpatrick? But, inappropriate. Beautiful couple. Honeymoon in Hawaii—Maui—the Kaanapali Beach Hotel." He chuckled. "They're probably lathering each other up with cocoa butter as we speak." He wiped his brow. "Wonderful couple, nice 'fits,' (with his fingers) and, okay, there, I've said it. Anyway, we thank them for the flowers."

Grace showed up for choir rehearsal that Wednesday at seven with Victoria in tow and was relieved to see there were a few other kids. In the succeeding weeks, Trinity Church became Grace's rock as she got to know a lot of warm and talented folks, including Gladys who was also the choir director. During rehearsals, Victoria and the other kids explored the haunted catacombs of the church, found the restroom under the stairs, the secret passage to the parsonage and, more than once, got seriously lost.

That Halloween they were hit with a rogue winter storm that broke out of the Arctic Circle splitting shipping lanes as it rolled down through Canada, sent Toronto underground, shattered windows and felled power lines in Buffalo and swept low in its arc for New York City. The full weight of the storm pummeled its broad shoulders into the stone walls of that Harrisburg church Wednesday night at nine o'clock. The lights hesitated and dimmed. Gladys checked her watch, closed her hymnal with a *Pop!* and said, "Time to get outta Dodge, people. Grace, round up Victoria, and you two ride with me."

"We'll take you up on that."

Grace insisted that Gladys not go out of her way with all the snow and one-way streets, so, with some push back, Gladys dropped them a block from their building.

"Wow!" Gladys said. The wind nearly took the passenger door. "You sure I can't drive you over?"

"We're fine, thanks." Grace gripped Victoria's hand firmly. "See ya Sunday." She slammed the door.

Gladys' car was whited out. There were three inches on the ground, and it was piling up fast as Grace and Victoria leaned into horizontal snow. Having second thoughts regarding Gladys' offer and more than a little disoriented, they had taken just a few steps when they were, from out of nowhere, smack square in the middle of high beams and a steaming chrome grill. The car slid up to within inches of them.

"Whoa there and damn, shit!" The large man in the uniform jumped out of the limo. "You okay?"

Grace wrapped herself around Victoria. The wind tried to drive whole flakes through her coat.

Another voice barely audible from inside the car, "Frederick, tell them to get in. All of you, get out of the storm and into the car!"

"C'mon, miss, come warm up. We'll take you wherever you want to go," the large man said. He hugged his shoulders, and his face showed signs of flash freezing.

Grace looked down. "What do you think?"

Victoria nodded.

The back door of the limo opened, and they piled blindly into white leather, cinnamon and deep, red carpets. The driver squeezed in behind the wheel and said to the mirror, "Boss, that's one mean storm out there."

"Oh my God!" Grace put her hand to her mouth. "You're Liberace!"

"Guilty as charged," he laughed.

"How, but, why, or what, I mean, you're—"

"Frederick, would you please crank up the heat back here? This poor woman is stuttering." He turned to them. "And, seeing how we almost made snow angels of you, I hope you'll call me Lee. My friends call me Lee."

"Lee." Grace nodded.

"There, that's better. You'll thaw in no time, honey." Four sparkling ringed fingers of his right hand bounced lightly off her knee. "As for us, we were driving over from Pittsburgh—of all places—on our way to Radio City Music Hall, then the storm and Frederick thought it might be a good idea to get lost in the middle of Harrisburg."

"The sign said 'I-81 this way,'" Frederick said to the mirror.

"Well, it sure ain't this way, now, is it, Frederick." He winked at Victoria. "I think our little sign maker elf meant the *other* this way."

Victoria giggled.

"So, here we are, lost in Harrisburg at ten o'clock at night and can't see past the end of the hood. Right, Frederick?"

"Yes sir, not past the end of the hood, and I got 9:56."

"Which way, dear?" Lee asked.

"Left. Oh, my, I'm sorry. I'm Grace. This is my daughter, Victoria. We're so very glad to meet you."

"Charmed, and you've already met our time-keeping navigator."

"Sir, we're going to have to stop for a while. I might as well be blind." A blast of snow blew in as he rolled down the window and took a swipe at the windshield.

"Here," Grace said. "This is it. Won't you please come in? For tea? You can wait it out with us."

"You are absolutely right, Grace. It would be a delight to get out of this for a bit, and we are honored to be your guests. Isn't that right, Frederick?"

"We are honored. Where shall I park?"

"There's a parking lot out back," Victoria said.

"Well, then." Lee flashed a family smile. "Let's not delay a moment longer."

Inside, they stomped off at the bottom of the stairs and shook the snow from their outer layers; Lee's was mink. Then, up the steps and into their apartment where Lee tossed the melting fur into the corner and immediately made himself comfortable with the Yamaha and Chopin. He patted the bench, and Victoria hopped up next to him.

Frederick followed Grace to the kitchen to raid the cupboards. He started the water for tea then arranged plates of cookies, apple slices and cheese. Grace went to her room, grinned into the mirror as she brushed her hair and tied her most decorative silk scarf loosely around her neck.

Frederick toted the tea, and Grace took the treats as they rejoined Lee and Victoria.

"One cookie, Victoria, then to bed."

"Yes mom, but I like playing the piano with Lee."

"She's a natural." Lee winked, pulling a flask from his pocket. "And, a little something to sweeten the tea, Frederick?"

"To sweeten the tea."

Grace tucked Victoria in. "I may be joining you in a little while, Victoria. If they want to stay, we'll let Lee have my bed, and Frederick can sleep on the couch."

"Sure, Mom. G'night."

Victoria lay awake listening to the story telling and the laughter through her door and they were at the piano and they were singing and their voices mixed and they were fading and the storm at her window...

"Every cloud must have a silver lining
Wait until the sun shines through
Smile my honey dear, while I kiss away each tear
Or else I shall be melancholy too."

By the piano that night with Frederick and Lee, Grace's skin stopped.

March 2001: *Francis Needs Wheels*

"Mom, we need a car." Francis thumped downstairs to the front room, his mother on the couch with a magazine and a *Phillies* pre-season game on TV. Out in the kitchen, sister Kathy rattled dishes in the sink.

"Mom?"

"Hey babe." Isabel waved, not looking up.

"We need a car."

"For what?"

"Like, for everything."

"Uh-huh. Whoa, inside corner! O and two."

"Really, mom, we should grow up and get a car. Look around. Everyone drives to work, to get groceries, to go to church, to get gas. We need a car."

"Whiff, you're outta there!" She looked up from the TV. "Sorry, Frankie, what?"

"I'm buying a car."

"Really. And, that would be with college money?"

"Yeah, I guess. But I'll replace it with a job I can drive to. Joey's quitting the bakery, and I can have his second shift, and Derrick Brothers have a used Corolla set aside for us. Toyotas are great!"

"A job, and a car and school, and when will I see you?"

"All the times I'm not waiting for the bus—you, too. You can drive to see your sister anytime you want. You can take a trip, we can go on vacation. We've never been on vacation."

"And, I guess you could pick up that girl? Kathy told me all about her, Francis. And, you'll be wanting to drive her to school and take her to the movies and there goes more money?"

His face went hot. "Uh, yeah, sure, Faye. Her name's Faye. And, why not?"

"Because she's a slut!" Kathy threw in from the kitchen.

"Stay out of this!" Francis spun and squared off.

"She is, and you know it!"

"Okay, children," Isabel said, pointing her finger. "Kathy?"

"Mom, you should see her. Nose in the air, doesn't talk to anyone, dates college guys."

"She doesn't date college guys." Francis said.

"Bottom of the ninth and Garciaparra is moved to short."

March 2001: *A Head-On Collision*

"Francis, next paragraph please? Francis?" Francis looked up from the book. "Will you read the next paragraph to the class, please?"

"I..." He blushed.

Victoria turned to the other side of the room. "Who will read the next paragraph?"

Defeated, Francis sat staring at the whiteboard. It wasn't that he cared about whatever it was they were reading, or the dangling prepositions, or moving the x or inverting the y. Like, what use was all of that, anyway? But, he did feel kind of bad about being such a fuck up, such a damned disappointment all the time. His school concentration wasn't as good as it had been before Christmas, and it wasn't great back then. But these past couple months his screws had further loosened, and he found himself wandering in dreams, attaching to anything that caught his eye for a moment, then spinning off again.

He was drawn back into what he had been reading from a different chapter than the rest of the class. It was a poem—something about feeling the pain of others, and maybe, second chances. He fell into its rhythm and disappeared.

At the end of class, his spell broken, books slammed shut, chairs scraped, and shoes, knees and elbows made for the door.

"Francis, could you wait a moment?" Victoria asked.

He stopped, turned and went back to her desk.

"I'm sorry to have embarrassed you today."

"It's okay, I lost my place."

"You've been distracted, with good reason."

"Yeah, sorry, I just—"

"Are you getting enough sleep?"

"Well, yeah, sure. I got a new job, so it's a little busy right now."

She went to the door and pulled it closed. Her hands behind her, she leaned against the door. She took a deep breath and paused. "Francis, we share something." She looked past him, out the window. "When I was six, I lost my father. He took his life."

Francis spun slowly and dropped into a desk in the front row. He closed his eyes.

"I'm sorry, Francis. I'm sorry for what's happened to you, and now I'm sorry I told you about my father. I had no right."

Neither of them heard the bell. In the hall, a riptide of students passed shoulder to shoulder. They squeezed from their flows and were sucked out and through the gates to their next classes. Victoria's was a planning period.

"Francis, I just want you to know that I care about you, about what happens here at school. I care about your future."

His books were stacked on the desk in front of him. He slid low in the seat. Seconds stretched to a minute.

She was doing a rapid search, looking for a way in, a way out. What could she say? He's a child, battered all his life, then this loss, this tragedy.

"Francis, you were in the back of our book when I called on you today. What were you reading?"

He looked up and breathed. "Oh, yeah, I don't know, a poem, I guess."

"Which poem?"

He shifted in the desk. "*Renascence*, a lady poet."

"Edna St. Vincent Millay."

"Yeah, that's it."

"What did you think of the poem?"

"It was okay, I guess. I don't know."

"What is the poem about?" She crossed the room to her desk. She would have to give him a note for his next class.

"I'm not sure; I didn't get it all."

"Which part did you get? Was there something that stood out?"

"I think it's about time travel, maybe, and how small we are, and like, there's so much pain out there and stuff we don't see."

"Commendable, Francis. I would like you to choose a passage, a portion of the poem and write about it tonight. This will be for extra credit." She wrote as she spoke. "Just explain what it means to you. You can leave your comments in my in-basket tomorrow. Here's a note for your next class. Now, go."

Victoria sat at her desk with the door closed for the rest of that period. She didn't do any planning.

March 2001: *Victoria Works Late*

"Hey, you're still here!" he yelled. "Shall I come back later?" Max rattled his cleaning cart into Victoria's room.

She'd heard him cleaning the room next door. More accurately, she heard what sounded like snorting, rutting and the churning up of linoleum, concrete and steel. It had a musical score—Texas flavored rock—and it was broadcast from the front of his cart and an oversize boombox. Max liked Stevie Ray Vaughn.

"I'm just finishing up, really," she said. "Please, go ahead with what you're doing."

"What? Sorry!" He stretched over the cart, turned down the music, straightened and removed yellow earplugs.

"I appreciate how this room looks each morning. The whole school, actually. You really make it shine."

He locked the wheels of the cart and leaned on it broad, with both hands. "I hope you're not—!" He adjusted his voice. "I hope you're not trying to flatter me, cause it's working."

Gray, sweat-patched T-shirt, Levis and she hadn't noticed his eyes and hair on the loading dock. Well, of course his eyes. Who has eyes like that—the Bahamas of blue? He'd been wearing a funny—okay, stupid—hat that day. Wool with too many earmuffs and zippers. A zippered forehead muff? Max had a close-cropped and perfectly cut flattop, the blond deck of an aircraft carrier. Leaning, there on his cart, he also had shoulders, and, on a rippled forearm, a bulldog tattoo.

She ran her knuckle across her upper lip. "I'm done here." She scurried papers into her bag, swiped her pen and pencils into her middle desk drawer and, as she stood, jammed her elbow on the back of her chair. "Ah!" She dropped back to her seat.

Max was at her side in an instant. "Ooo, that sucks. Crazy bone. I hate that!" He held her arm with both hands and helped her up. "Pump."

"I'm sorry?"

"Your arm. Pump it hard. Flex it, you know?" He kept one hand on her shoulder and lowered the other to her wrist as she tried to escape. "Walking's good, but just keep flexing your arm—and elevated. Here, like this." He pulled her wrist high. "The pain'll stop. Pump, pump, pump." He walked her to the door and, with a solid pat on the back, released her.

It was a long, dark, mirror-polished hall, and from her door and all the way to the end, she heard him, "Pump, pump, pump." She pumped until she was out of sight.

"He's exhausting."

The Song of Aphrodite, *or was it maybe Prende?*

It was the Monday after the hip-throw book scattering that Faye touched his desk as she passed. Francis was seated, ready for class, and, in all the pre-class noise, she passed and for not even a second lightly touched the tips of the fingers of her left hand to the edge of his desk. The spot smoldered: long, tapered fingers bronzed in the Eastern sun, fingers he imagined trailing their silent wake behind a carved-out canoe and splitting the blood-red pulp of exotic fruit with their strong grip and the back of her narrow hand a smooth rolling plain of golden satin. The ring. On her index finger, the one that might firmly stop him in his tracks or seductively invite him closer, on that finger was a delicate gold band that trapped a small aquamarine sphere. On Tuesday, she was absent. Wednesday, she touched his desk again, and that night at the bakery Natalie, the foreman, asked, "Can we expect you to be taking your head out of your ass anytime soon, Sugar?" On Friday, he made his move.

It wasn't like he'd just cooked it up. He'd been stewing for days. If he was to ask her out, and it made his palms sweat every time he thought about it, which was much of the time, it couldn't be somewhere they'd be seen. That wouldn't work for him, and it surely wouldn't be what she'd want. No movies, concerts, eating in public or bowling. Anyway, he hated bowling—like, those shoes. She must think it was pretty lame, too. The drive-ins didn't open for another month, besides which, suggesting that would be too slimy and the end of any possibility of him and her forever. No, they had to get out of here. He could drive her up to Eagle's Mere, and they could hike around the lake and rent a boat. Or, he could show her the view from the pinnacle at Hawk Mountain. Yeah, nobody went there. Hawk Mountain!

At the end of class, Friday, he slipped a note under his arm, behind him and slid it onto her desk. She took it, and he never thought a weekend could pass so slowly.

From three to eight each night he packed loaves of bread, hot dog rolls or hamburger buns, depending on what they were baking, into boxes for shipping out to the region's grocery stores. He was to count as he packed, thirty-six loaves per box, twenty-four packs of rolls. Grab a flat box, unfold it, tape the bottom and start packing. Meanwhile, the loaves had been backing up on the conveyor as he "diddly-fucked" with the box. Those were his foreman's—Natalie's—words. The bakery had thrown him into the deep end of what would happen if he didn't finish high school and go on to college. Examples abounded: Larry Hazzard—dumpy, pale and thirty-something Big Larry—who delivered the flat boxes to his station and told him how "fuckin stupid" he was and who still lived at home with his five brothers and a sister and his aunts and uncles and cousins and a dozen-or-so scatter-brained dogs having litters twice as fast as their masters at what looked like a salvage yard at the end of the valley that for as-long-as anyone could remember had been known as The Hazzard Compound. Another example was Skinny Sheryl. Skinny Sheryl Hazzard, Larry's little sister in jungle boots, wife-beater shirt, blue Mohawk and a thousand piercings. Sheryl did nothing but stand and watch about a million loaves of white bread pass by on the conveyor belt for a third of her life and tell on him every time he didn't get the loaves into boxes fast enough.

"Sheryl, I'm trying, I really am," he'd said.

"Yeah, you're trying my patience, you candy-ass dick wad!"

Sheryl was scary. She didn't just yell. She once pinned him against the wall and put a knife to his throat. The knife was awful, but her breath was worse. The hardest part of the job was keeping Skinny Sheryl's yelling mouth out of his face every night.

And, Natalie. Red-headed, short-shorted and always-talking-sex, Natalie. The foreman.

"Natalie, the belt's stuck."

"That's what he said."

"Natalie, can I take a bathroom break?"

"Only if I can hold it, short stroke."

The noise, the dust and the numbing tempo at the bakery were welcome distractions, great time killers as his nerves hurdled toward that next Saturday when he hoped to drive the just-waxed Corolla up her drive, knock on the door and greet her face-to-her-beautiful-face. Following a sleepless weekend, it was back to school and work Monday, another anxiety-filled night tossed in the strangling sheets and school and work Tuesday. It was during Tuesday night's drive home that Francis finally dozed off, drifted through a stop sign and caused an elderly gentleman great alarm as he plowed his cherry, '64 white Caddie into the Corolla's rear quarter panel, ripped of its bumper and sent the crushed Toyota spinning up over the curb and onto the front walk of Knowle's Funeral Chapel. When the car came to rest, there was additional damage as Francis first reacted to the event by leaving a significant fist print on the padded dash. Francis and the elderly gentleman were late getting home that night.

The next morning, Faye dropped a note onto his desk with her number and, "Call today, 4:15." The breath sucked out of him, panicked and depressed, and his hand throbbed. His car was messed up! It could have worked— her note, and all. But, now his car. 4:15? He'd be at the bakery. Natalie would be all over his case. She didn't miss a thing. It would work. He'd make it work. He'd call her at 4:15 from the phone in the restroom.

She Bribes Him with Cookies

Ms. Merritt caught him, again, at the end of class. "Francis, a word?"

Now what?

"It may seem as though I'm picking on you. I'm not. I see you as a sensitive, caring young man, and that sets you apart from many. You have a lot going on in your life, right now, immeasurable pressures."

I gotta get to P.E., and what's she talking about?

"I'd like to help you manage, here, for a while, to help keep you on track until things return to a less strenuous status."

Less strenuous?

"Ms. Sweeney has suggested that perhaps you and I could meet a couple times a week for ten minutes before school to see how your work is progressing, to help keep your school calendar in order and to just check in with each other."

This is supposed to help? Another *thing*? He stared at the floor. "I'm okay, really. I mean, thanks, but, like, I'm already seeing a counselor a couple times a week and I'm doing fine, he says, and—"

"Tuesdays and Thursdays at 7:50. I'll bring the cookies."

A Payphone in the Restroom?

"Natalie, I'm feeling sick. Gotta go to the restroom. Soon!" Francis said.

"Larry, take over young stud's station for a few. Go for it, ding-a-ling, then, you owe me."

He dashed into the huge empty john and, weirdly, the closest phone. His watch said, "4:14." He dropped a couple quarters and punched in her number. Two rings and she answered.

"Hey." He wished his voice didn't sound like he was in a crapper, which she could probably tell right away. He tried putting the phone into the crux of his elbow. "So, you're home."

"I just wanted to thank you for my books, the other day. That was nice. Sweet, okay?"

"Oh, yeah, well—"

"So, I have to go, but thanks," she said.

"No, I mean, wait." Breathe, breathe! "Did you read my note? Can we do something together, like, this weekend, Saturday? I can show you a cool place not too far from here—Hawk Mountain. There's tons of hawks and eagles soaring, and it's a cool hike, and I'll pack a lunch for us. You like turkey or ham? And we'd be home early if that'd be okay, and no one has to know, and all, and I have a car." He was at ten-thousand feet and pointed face down. The earth approached at the speed of gravity.

Natalie banged on the restroom door. "Hey Slick Willie, you fall in, or what?"

Toward the door, "Be right out!"

"Sorry about that, I'm at work. The foreman's all over my case." The phone was quiet. God, he was a fool! Like, ham or turkey? What the...? "Are you still there?" he asked.

"Yes, I'm here. I'll be at the Circle K at two. Bye." Dial tone.

He replayed it in his head, "Yes I'm here," and, "Circle K at two." He hung up, went into a stall, flushed the toilet and shuffled over to the deep mop sink. He doused his face, then stuck his head all the way under. He straightened up, smiled at no one, shook his head and sprayed like a dog.

Dripping, he returned to his workstation. "I'm okay, Big Larry, thanks." He slapped Larry on the back, and for the rest of the shift and beneath curious eyes he packed hot dog buns like it was his own late-night show.

The Date

The crushed Corolla looked like it was in a constant rear end slide, and Francis had been given a fix-it ticket. But, it drove okay. They'd be able to make it out to Hawk Mountain. He pulled into the Circle K at two sharp. Faye came out of the store, got into the car and locked the door seamlessly before he had switched off the motor.

"Hey," he offered turning in his seat.

"Hey," to the windshield.

Was it from the radio, the rippled sounds of a deep jungle pool? High above, monkeys screeched across cascading falls, parrots shrieked their delight and, far off, that might have been Tarzan's call. He sat fixed. He searched up and down his dial. What to say?

"So, I guess we'll go, then, to Hawk Mountain?" she asked.

"Yes." It was a couple seconds until he regained signal. He shouldn't have done this. Way out of his league. She was just being nice because he picked up her books. Probably still had a really serious boyfriend at that other school. Probably some huge guy that, if he saw him here with her right now, the guy'd love to punch him between the eyes.

He turned into the tall weeds up the dirt road from the official parking lot avoiding the ranger fee and shut off the car. He reached over and pulled his daypack from the back seat. "The back door doesn't work right now." He thought he saw a hint of a smile. Getting snagged a few times, they followed a rabbit path a couple hundred yards through the brambles to the main trail. Neither of them was dressed for forest adventure, at least from an L.L. Bean point of view. He wore jeans, beaten-down Chuck Taylors and a Ramones sweatshirt. She was, like, from another place: skinny green jeans, a tightly-fit, short, purple velvet Chinese-looking jacket and scuffed brown boots that laced to her knees.

Looking back over his shoulder, she seemed to know what she was doing—at home in the woods. He should say something. He swallowed hard and tried for speech, started a couple sentences under his breath, and it wasn't working. It was like his mouth had just been to the dentist. He should tell her how great she looked or how happy he was they were—that he couldn't believe they were here, that she was—like, friggin beautiful, and he was already in love and he was a nervous dork. Probably best to just keep quiet and keep walking.

Twenty minutes into the ascent they emerged to a vast sunbaked radiant boulder field and began lizard-hopping up and across from rock to rock. Near the middle of the field he stopped. "Wait here." He bounced off to the tree line on their right. Moments later he was back with two ice-cold Pepsis. Taking one, she looked at him sideways. He laughed. "I keep a stash in a spring up here."

She nodded and sipped.

I keep a stash in a spring up here, he thought. I keep a stash in a spring up here because I'm a nerd who would think of such a thing is probably what she's thinking. He jammed the crushed empties into his pack, and they were off through the laurel to the summit. Heaving, they broke into the clearing at the top. He led her over to the view.

"Amazing, isn't it?"

"Yes." She moved closer behind him. They stood quiet and cast thoughts to the distance.

"Makes you feel so small. I mean, look how far you can see and nothing but more mountains. This place makes you forget stuff."

"Stuff?"

"You know, mistakes, all the pressure and everything."

She stepped next to him, her shoulder lightly against his and a current passed between them. "You don't have to say anything about your father," she said.

"I don't—"

"You don't."

They were quiet; just the wind. "Right," he said. "Right." Cloud shadows raced over the forests below them like time-lapse photography. "See those two hawks spiraling up the thermal? Down there? Way out, down over there?" He pointed.

"I see them."

"If we stand here for half-an-hour, we'll see loads more. Eagles and falcons, too."

"But, we can't. We have to go."

He turned to her, "But, I—"

"Really, Francis, my father. I have to get back." She focused squarely on him for the first time, and something in his gut collapsed and his knees weren't holding.

"Yeah, well, okay. Let's go, then."

Senses sharpened, they didn't speak during the descent. They sweated. Their pulses matched. Their breath mixed in the thick solitude on that narrow trail of broken rock. Slipping, regaining, he grabbed her shoulder for balance, and she caught his arm to steady— the birds, the insects and the rustle of their clothing.

Finally, on the flats he said, "Well, the car's still here and no ticket." They climbed in with rubber legs and sank into the Toyota's seats. He wrestled the wheel as the car lurched out through ruts and weeds. "There're other places like this. Maybe go to Eagles Mere next week, or Ricketts Glen. There's a huge canyon north of here that you can hike for days and—"

"Francis, I don't know. Maybe. Sometimes you can't plan. This is good: the hike, the hawks, the soda."

"We could—"

"Let's not talk, now, okay?"

"Right, I'll take you home."

"The Circle K. I'll walk from there."

"But—"

"Francis."

Yep, he thought. Just being nice—a one and out. What was he thinking? Look at her! Fool.

In the parking lot, she opened the door, reached over and touched his knee before stepping out, "Thank you. This was nice."

"Yeah, me too."

Fix It

Monday, Francis had worked late. On his drive home, a deputy stopped him on the dark creek road and encouraged him to have his bumper and taillight fixed asap.

The deputy leaned against his cruiser and unscrewed a bottled water. "Frankie, this can't go on forever." He took a long swig, "Go to the Sebastian brothers. They're cheap, and they'll do it right away. Talk to Fred. They know your uncle Bobby. So, how's your mom?"

Francis was going to call Faye again. He couldn't eat for the next two days, and he started to dial a dozen times but hung up before the first ring. He paced in the front room. What did he have to lose? She could only say, "No," and that would be that. He'd go back to being a nothing— a nothing with no hope and having to hear about it from Kathy, and she'd probably tell all her friends, and if she did—well, he didn't know what except that it would be awful. He could just leave it as it is, just be happy they went out once. He should. He dialed again.

The following Saturday at two, Francis picked Faye up at the Circle K, and they drove up the pike to The Turkey Ranch where he paid for shakes and fries to go. Opening their bags, they sat leaning against the car in the creek-side grass and talked about their teachers, the homework and his job.

"And, Natalie, let me tell you. She's the foreman, and she's witch-scary. Always right behind you when you don't know it, and she'll goose you every chance she gets. You smell her before you see her—her perfume. All dyed red hair, and bracelets, and earrings, and her tight little shorts and everything. It's weird. She's like, so old, you know? I mean, not like grandma, or anything, but old."

"Her tight little shorts," Faye said.

He blushed. "I mean she's like, I don't know, just over the top, you know?"

"Her shorts?"

"No, I mean, yeah, her, well, she's—"

She smiled. "I'm sorry, Francis. Great shakes."

He wiped his mouth with the back of his hand. "Yeah, they do a good job. So, I guess you don't like being here that much. The school, and all."

"It is what it is."

"You've moved around a lot?"

"Yes."

"I've never moved, always stuck right here. Same town, same faces, same bedroom window. I wish we had a dog, or I played piano, or I was taller or something." He took a pull on his straw. "I wish we could move, like, someplace cool. I mean, like France or New Jersey. Somewhere with an ocean. You know, none of us: my mom, my sister or me, ever saw the ocean? Where'd you like it best?"

"I liked being with my mother."

"Oh, I—"

"Things change, we change. She wasn't supposed to die." Faye stared at the creek.

"Oh, yeah, I—my mom—like, my dad. Yeah, things change." They sat in the still for minutes, almost never a car on the creek road.

"So, Francis, here we are, stuck without an ocean."

"Hey, let's go see about getting this car fixed, okay?"

"Okay, let's do that."

They jumped in and, pulling away, Francis cranked up Zep's *Whole Lotta Love.*

Francis edged the little Toyota through the depressed one-story neighborhood and up the narrow driveway between the Sebastian brothers' house-turned-body-shop and the towering fenced hedgerow separating it from their neighbor. With little room to open his door, he asked Faye, "Wait here a sec?"

He squeezed past the front of the car and approached the looming chain-link fence at the head of the drive. Reaching out to the gate, he retracted his hand midair as two sleek, black, canine missiles arrived waist-high on the other side and emitted barely audible growls. They dared him.

"Hold on, there, Peaches. Back off, Raider; relax now." Fred Sebastian's twelve-foot shadow preceded his six-foot-five to the gate. The Dobermans retreated across packed dirt to a neutral corner of what looked like a prison yard: chin up bar, basketball hoop, weight bench with scattered plates all around, tumbled and rusted auto body parts and, oddly, a one-third-scale gingerbread and ornately-painted Victorian house in the rear corner. Fred unchained the gate, swung it open and motioned an unsmiling, "In!" with his head. Francis passed beneath him. Fred was about to re-chain the gate, then stopped. He dropped the chain and walked the few yards down the drive to the car and motioned for Faye. She grinned, climbed over to the driver's side and slid out. The dogs remained on alert by the weight bench. Francis hadn't given a thought to blinking. "Come on in out of the sun," Fred welcomed Faye. "Check out the puppies if you like. They're in a box back there in the bike shed past the barber chair. Peaches won't mind, will you, Peaches?"

Fred watched as Faye led the dogs across the baked dirt.

"Now." He turned a stone face down to Francis, crossed his arms and stared.

Francis cleared his throat. "My car's smashed, and my uncle said maybe you could fix it."

"Your uncle."

"Uncle Bobby, er, Robert Thomas. Deputy Thomas."

"Which one?"

He cleared his throat and swallowed hard, "Sheriff's Deputy Robert Thomas."

"Don't know him. What's wrong with your car?"

"The rear end got hit, the bumper's off, the tail light's gone and the rear doors and trunk won't open."

Fred nodded.

"So, is it fixable? I mean, is it expensive?"

"Dunno."

"I— Would you want to have a look?"

Fred's stare twisted into him for a few painful seconds. He stepped past Francis, opened the gate, went down the drive, squeezed around the car and assessed the situation.

"What do you think?" Francis called.

Fred returned, ignored Francis and went into the bike shed. Inside, Fred said something, and Faye laughed.

Francis stood alone in the sun as Faye and Fred crossed the yard and were joined by another large biker-looking guy—a broader, gnarlier version of Fred. As puppies yelped in the background and old-time gospel music drifted from the used-to-be bedroom, Fred began his tour of the Victorian pigeon coop. "Faye, they got babies in here, all hidden. Their mamas don't like us lookin at em, but what are they gonna do? When we open the doors, they just leave em anyway. It's how they're built. They come back, but they leave em first, fly around in circles, maybe light on the wires, then they always come back. Right Lou?"

"Right," Lou said. "We took em far from here once. Let em out, then we sped home on the bikes, my brother on the Glide and me on that there FXR. Dint stop, kept our foot in it near a ton fer a hunert miles and damn birds beat us home. Who'd think? Lost one bird, though. They say hawks get em. Fast birds, hawks."

Fred flushed the birds from the coop. "Francis, look!" Faye called. They were like a school of airborne shimmering fish whipping left, then right, up, over, around and diving, white on one side and soaring mirrors on the other. The racing squadron circled wide until, on a silent signal, the birds landed on the wires above the yard fussing, nudging, picking and purring.

Faye, Francis and Lou watched as Fred made a move toward the coop door, tapped it twice with a tin cup and the birds whooshed in like being sucked down a straw. They made a hell of a clatter finding their little cubbies. Fred closed the door.

"There you go, dear. That's what they like to do."

Francis gathered his nerves and stepped closer to them. "So, what do you think, I mean, can you fix it? My car"

Now, the brothers gave him their full attention, and Francis felt surrounded. Fred, to the side, staring down into his ear and Lou, front and center, dust mask around his muscular neck and thick white hair showing sixty years of havoc. Lou's lips barely moved. "You need a car fixed?"

"Yes, I, uh—"

"What's wrong?"

Francis glanced up at Fred, then quickly back center, "Er, it got smashed in back. Can you fix it?"

"Don't know, have to look," Lou said.

Francis waited a few awkward seconds thinking, So? "Would now be an okay time? I mean, to look?"

Lou glanced toward the driveway, then back at Francis. "Guess so." Hands in his back pockets, he moseyed to the car.

Francis turned to Fred who motioned toward Lou with his head and raised eyebrows implying, "Well?" Francis joined Lou as he examined the Toyota, front to rear. At the back of the mangled car, Lou pulled half a pipe out of his jeans pocket, checked the bowl and lit up. Smoke climbed his face as he contemplated the situation. He cocked his head, scratched his shoulder, stooped for a while and finally asked, "What hit the dash?"

Francis' eyes dropped. "I guess I did that."

"Six hunert."

"Six hundred?! Geesh! I'm just a kid, and I gotta pay for this out of my own pocket, or my insurance will go crazy!" Francis squawked. He realized, immediately, he may have overreacted.

Lou emptied his pipe against the heel of his boot, stuck it back in his jeans and started toward the gate.

"Um, I mean, sure, six hundred." Francis followed.

Lou stopped abruptly and turned. Francis' color fled. "You see?" One eye squinting, the opposite eyebrow raised, Lou engaged his hammer and anvil hands for emphasis. "First I have to break it down, then pound, pull and bend back to shape what can be pount, pullt and bent. Then, what's been ripped and trashed so bad it can't be bent back to shape has to be got from a parts place. Til the new parts get here, I'll sand, prime, paint and shine the bent parts that I just got done with. If, and when, the new parts get here from Tie Won or Ill Noise or some such place, I'll put the whole mess back so it looks new, but your light still don't work. Last, I'll fix that. Then, the back of your car will look as good as the front of your car, and I still ain't fixed that dash. Six hunert still sound like too much?"

"No, I mean, it's a lot, but it sounds like a lot of work, too."

"You in school?"

"Yeah, senior."

"Dad work?"

"My mom does, my dad's—"

"You got a job?"

"Yeah."

"Where?"

"Topmann's Bakery, second shift, twenty-five hours a week."

"Five hunert. Two hunert up front, and pay as you go."

"Great! Yeah, thanks. Deal," Francis said. They shook. "Is that your Harley?"

Another Late Night

Victoria had heard him. How could she not? He cleaned his way, room-by-room toward hers, and she was proud of herself for closing shop, turning off the lights and leaving while Max was still two rooms away. He made her nervous with his touching—he had touched her twice, now—his self-confidence and standing too close looking straight into her eyes. She walked purposely down the far side of the hall, then eased her steps. Darn! He appeared in a doorway. She stopped.

"Workin late again, eh?" he yelled over the music.

"Hello, Max." She felt her color rise. "Yes, I've just finished."

"Goin home, then?"

"Yes, tomorrow is another day."

"Sure is. Nother dollar. You walk to work, huh?"

"I take the bus from my house, actually, to the bottom of the hill. I walk from there."

"Yeah, I see you walking up and down the hill. You look a lot like a nun most times, all black, white and grey. Not a nun, though. Am I right?"

Is there anyone else in the building? She thought. Surely they hear this. "I—"

"More like still waters run deep, if I had my guess. You know, you can't tell a book, and all that?"

"Of course."

"You getting used to this place?"

"Yes, thank you."

"Must be hard, being new and all."

"I am adjusting."

He disappeared from the doorway. She took another two steps, the music stopped, and he was back. "So, you've made your way around? Seen the town, checked things out?"

"I'm finding my way."

"Been to the museum?"

"I haven't."

"Art galleries on Third Street?"

"No."

"You dance?"

"I— No, and I'm sorry, I must be going."

"Don't want to miss your bus."

"No."

"That pump work? Take care of what ails you?"

"I'm sorry?" she asked. This is ridiculous. Just go.

"Your arm. The crazy bone. You banged it?"

"Oh, yes, of course. Quite effective, thank you. Bye, now. It's been nice chatting with you." She was five doors down the hall when she heard him again.

"Maybe we could grab a bite sometime, you and me."

The Kiss

Time crawled for Francis. He saw Faye only in English class and at lunch. Weekends were out since that Saturday they left Francis' car with the Sebastians and took the bus back to the Circle K. Francis had, against Faye's better judgment, walked her up the valley to within a hundred yards of her house.

"This is already too close. You're sweet, but go now. I'll see you Monday." In the fading light, she had placed her hands on his chest, kissed his cheek and disappeared.

Something went seriously out of round at the base of his spine, rolled off the truck and rattled down around the horn. For a few moments, he wasn't sure where he was, or if he was, and was he standing or sitting? He raised his fingers to his cheek. It felt different than before, his cheek. It was cool and teaberry-peppermint, his cheek. And, now it was on his fingers. He put them to his lips, and it was like the time he'd touched his tongue to the nine-volt battery. He didn't move from that spot in the road until— he didn't know how long. Darkness dropped. He heard creaking. What's that? Crickets? Man, they're loud out here. He spun around. Where *is* here?

Faye's Story

Faye and Francis agreed he shouldn't call her. They had to go dark until enough time passed for her dad to cool down from seeing the kiss. He'd been cleaning inside the lion's cage, glanced out through the gate and saw her kiss Francis. It hadn't gone well between Faye and her father that night.

So, it was to be only school and work for both of them: him boxing loaves for the bakery and her stacking wood for her dad. At school, things had improved for Faye since it was known that she and Francis were a thing. The cheerleaders and divas still didn't speak to her, but none of them were "accidentally" bumping into her or jamming her locker. The boys remained their awkward selves.

Two weeks after the kiss, they met Saturday at two at the Circle K. The Toyota looked like new, and she jumped in. They sat quiet for a moment.

"Your car looks great."

"Oh. Yeah. Thanks."

They sat, Francis in wonderland.

"To the Turkey Ranch?" she asked.

"Oh, sure."

They leaned against the car in the grass along the creek, opened their bags, lifted out the famously thick shakes and drove extra wide straws through squealing lids.

"Dad wasn't always so over-protective, but, now, I'm all he has. He cuts top wood left by loggers and I help. Saturdays, we start at five in the morning and work until noon stacking what he's cut and split all week. He makes deliveries the rest of the day and Sundays. I have a list of chores that I speed through quicker than he thinks. Chores to keep me too busy for boys. For you."

"Where's your mom?"

Faye lowered her shake next to Francis'.

"He and mom were beautiful together. He made her laugh, and she sang to him. Armend and Maya Baris, his thick black hair, and she was dark, quiet. She moved like a cat."

"Like you," he said.

"They toured Europe with a small show, *Buzuku Mystik*. Dad worked his way on a freighter to Africa and brought back a lion cub, Jono. He trained him, loved him as a son. They chose Tsunami as their show names. Armend and Maya Tsunami."

"Like the storm," Francis said.

"The sign painter was unaware of the silent T. In the end, we were the Sunamis."

"There's a T?"

"I was the pet of the show: the drivers, the clowns and jugglers, my crazy dog trainer uncle, the musicians, acrobats, hucksters. Mom and Auntie Edona, Mom's younger sister. They taught me to cook while they schooled me in languages, histories and geography. Learning was fun then, a game. They left arithmetic to old Afrim. He had a computer in his head and was lightning fast. He showed me the simple purity, the elegant language of numbers and how to roll a rube." Faye scooted forward into the sun. Francis remained.

She told Francis about an early morning in San Marcos, Calabria, the trucks and wagons in a circle at the church commons. Some of the locals had gathered around the magician in his sneakers and sweats, and he performed simple coin tricks to their amusement. They were welcome and happy, and all was warmth and smiles until one of the villagers led his four large dogs too close to Jono's cage. The dogs went wild with their barking and lunging. The owner encouraged them. Jono paced, roared, whipped his tail and smashed at the bars with his paws. Her dad raced over, "Get back! Get away!"

The man laughed, "Is pussy cat."

"Get away. Now!"

The man cursed and pulled his dogs back and away.

Francis moved their shakes out of the sun and into the shade beneath the car.

"By noon, the ring was set up, the flags and banners and the ropes strung to keep the crowd at a safe distance. My father led Jono on his chain down the ramp for the run-through before the performance. The dogs were back, untethered and crazy. They surrounded Jono. He pulled from Dad's grip, grabbed one of the dogs and broke its back. The other three spun away and into the church. Jono went after them. From inside the church, there were awful sounds. Then, Jono came out, blood on his face and mane. He dragged his chain, the only sound."

The commons lay empty and quiet. Light and shade moved across its stone surface like slow, intersecting streams as her dad led Jono to the truck.

"Dad took Jono's chain and led him up the cage ramp. He said something quiet to Jono, swung the door closed and reached for the bolt. Behind us—the man. He had a rifle. He said, 'Now I kill cat.'"

Francis sat straighter against the car.

"My father turned and started down the ramp. The man raised the gun. 'Maybe I shoot you, too, fica.' Mom pushed me behind her and moved up to the side of the ramp, closer to Dad. Dad told the man, 'No, you won't do that.' He raised his hand to my mother, 'Maya, stay.' The man shot, and Dad fell. The cage door snapped open and caught mom on the side of her head. Jono landed on the man and crushed him into the stones. It happened so fast, and it was over. Auntie held me, everyone crying, screaming. My father lay bleeding. The bullet shattered his hip. My mother was dead."

"Faye, I'm sorry." Francis edged into the sun next to her.

"That was seven years ago. Things fell apart. Dad and I came to America. We traveled around the South for a while with him picking up work, here and there. He was different, always on guard, arguing, fighting. He thought maybe we'd hire on to a circus in Florida or Arizona, but I guess we had too much baggage with Dad being Dad and me tagging along. No one wanted us, so we kept moving. He decided there was no life here, he'd go back to Albania. He'd help rebuild, break up the corruption, get Jono back."

"But he didn't. I mean, you're still here."

"He went back. I stayed with my aunt." She stood and leaned, her back against the car.

Francis looked up to her and shielded his eyes. "But, didn't you just move here? Like, this semester?"

"I was a handful that first year, for my aunt and everyone around me. I was sent to a special school. Now that I've reformed, and Dad's back, I guess I'm considered normal."

"You were at reform school?"

"Yes."

"What was that like? I mean it had to be—"

"I didn't adapt very well."

"And you have a lion?"

"Jono."

"In a cage? Like, that's okay?"

"Each night, Dad walks him up over the ridge. There's an endless series of meadows on the other side. Jono hunts."

"Damn."

Francis got up, took a dozen steps—roots and rocks—down to the water and sat. The creek was alive. Birds hopped from branch to branch, insects streaked above the current, the low, backlit leaves flashed and glowed above and around him. And, the water. The water flowing past this moment had started its journey far from here, a trickle from beneath a rock, maybe months ago—months ago before his dad—before his life changed. Minutes passed. They could come for him any time. They may be on the phone with his mom this very second. He felt Faye's hand on his shoulder. She knelt by him, her other hand on his knee.

"Francis," she followed his stare to the water, "I know about you. It's crazy, but sometimes—not always, but sometimes—I see. Things are bad, then we move on."

Victoria and Francis: 7:53am

"I got the letter. I'm enrolled at City College. Summer. Developmental classes to get me up to speed for fall. No one in our family's ever been to college. Mom and everyone expects me to be something special. But, my grades, well, you know. Big Larry's the dumbest guy at the bakery, and he reminds me how stupid I am every night. He hates me cause I'm so stupid. Says I'm dumber than a bag of—well, you name it. The two of them work me over pretty good, him and his sister, Sheryl. She says I couldn't find my di— Er, whatever. Anyway, me getting through City College doesn't look so good."

"Francis, have a cookie. Chocolate chip." Victoria pushed the plate further across her desk. "I apologize that we have never talked about the passage you chose from *Renascence*. It's a long poem. Why those lines?"

"Oh, yeah, well, I don't know." He took a cookie. "Some of it I didn't get, and some of it was kinda creepy, but I got a feeling from that part, I guess."

"What feeling, Francis?"

"You know, like feeling sorry for what happens to people and just not being able to do anything about it." He took a bite.

"A helpless feeling?"

"Yeah, like watching the news, you know?"

"Hopeless?"

"No, she made it better in the end, that poet. Like in the movies. Like, everything's hard and explosions and the bad guy, then everyone's happy and everything's going to be alright. The movies."

"But, life's not like that?"

"I don't think so. But, hey, what do I know?"

"So, life's helpless, hopeless?" Victoria asked.

He fussed with his cuffs, pulled his jacket down at the waist and concentrated on his sneakers. "I guess there's no going back. Maybe I wouldn't if I could, anyway." He looked up at her. "But, college? That's going to be a challenge."

"This is a difficult year for you. You're doing barely acceptable work, but you will improve. The worst you will do in this class is a C. Let's not give up on college, okay?"

"Sure, right." He was back at his sneakers.

"Francis, look at me. We're getting through this, okay?"

Now she was staring at him. Waiting. Like, she's already here, he thought. Already made it. Like, an adult, a teacher behind the desk and good pay, and she makes the rules and all that stuff she teaches, and she knows a lot and everything's good. You can't get there from here. That's something she doesn't know. He thought maybe she wanted him to nod, or something.

"Francis, take a cookie-to-go. I'll see you in an hour."

From "Renascence" – Edna St. Vincent Millay:
My anguished spirit, like a bird,
Beating against my lips I heard;
Yet lay the weight so close about
There was no room for it without.
And so beneath the weight lay I
And suffered death, but could not die.

Best Zucchini Ever

"So, Victoria, how's it going with you and Francis?" Marge asked. She trolled a fried zucchini stick through ranch dressing. "You guys friends?"

"How's his sister? And, their mother?"

"Kathy's doing well, and Isabel is glowing. They've been joined at the hip for years: daughter and mother. Their bond's different now—not defensive, not circling the wagons. They're finding their wings."

"Francis is good with me," Victoria said. "I'd say we're friendly heading toward friends. I bake him cookies, and he's started opening up some. I don't think it's the cookies, though."

"No?" Marge waved to the bartender.

"No, he has a new influence in his life. Someone special, strong."

"You're special and strong."

"Not like her, Marge. The Sunami girl, Faye, is one in a million, and she and Francis have found each other. If it was just Francis, I'd say puppy love, but not with Faye. There's something different about her, dark. He's growing up quickly since they're together. Too quickly."

"Victoria— Oh, hey, thanks handsome." The bartender placed two glasses and picked up the empties. "And, you were right." Marge dipped the tip of her finger into the dressing, held it erect and licked. "Best zucchini ever." He smiled and went back to the bar. She turned to Victoria. "By the way, there's talk around the school that a certain custodian has your number, not that it's anyone's business. But, it's a newsy school, and has your color just changed?"

Victoria sat straighter. "I really don't know how to respond to that."

"Just another rumor then."

"Yes."

"He's cute though, isn't he? Never married. Just a few years older than you."

"I really couldn't say how old Max is."

"Max."

Why a Raft?

"G'morning Ms. Merritt."

"You've got a lift in your step this morning, Francis." She closed her drawer.

"Yep, got my car back together. The Sebastians did a great job. Like new. Even cleaned the interior."

"Sebastians?"

"Yeah, Fred and Lou, body shop guys, hardcore bikers. Gotta keep an eye on Lou, kinda scary. Not exactly mean, but he never smiles. They have a soft spot for Faye, especially Fred. Showed her the puppies and his pigeons." Francis sat in the chair across the desk from her. "Says if we ever run into trouble, just give a call. Like, he'll straighten it out—him and Lou—like our bodyguards, or something. Weird, huh?"

"Fred has pigeons."

"Yep, Homing Pigeons—white—about forty of em in a coop at their place. They can reach a hunert miles-an-hour."

She pushed the plate of cookies toward him and poured herself another coffee. "Hunert?"

"That's what Lou says, 'near a hunert.' Your weekend good?"

"Good, yes, thank you." She stirred her cup.

"So, like, whatta you do weekends, like grade papers and stuff? You probably read a lot, huh?"

"Yes, I grade papers and read. Sometimes I stare forlornly out the window at the frolicking young people and wish I could go outside."

"Huh?"

"I am teasing, Francis. This weekend, I went to the farmers' market and visited the county museum. Have you been there, to the museum? There's quite a lot of history, here, with the Native Americans, the logging, the music culture. Maybe you and Faye will go sometime."

"Oh, right."

"Are things still good with you two?"

Francis was quiet for a moment, his gaze out the window. "She's magic."

Both hands, she lowered her cup to the desk. "Really. How so?"

"She just has a way about her, like sometimes she knows things—like a wizard—before they happen, like, I don't know, and she's lived all over the world and seen things—hard things—bigger than here. She speaks three languages. You know?"

"No, I did not know."

"And, we don't have to talk at all. Sometimes we can be quiet together and it's okay. I mean, we sit and watch the creek and we're just being."

"Have you met her parents? Or, she your mother?"

"No, maybe it's too soon. We don't really talk about that. Her dad's private, stays to himself and my mom's life is good right now except for the county, and all."

"The investigation."

"Yeah. I guess it's over. That's what Bobby says."

"Bobby?"

"My uncle. He's a deputy."

"I'm glad that it's over. And, you're doing an excellent

job maintaining your life and supporting your mother and sister."

"I guess." He looked up at the clock, gathered his books and stood. "Gotta get going. See ya in an hour."

That weekend Victoria stood on the dike overlooking the river and, beyond that, the city. This was the first she'd been behind her house.

He was comfortable talking to her. It was happening. He was okay talking about the investigation, Faye, her dad, his mom.

How did they just sit and watch water flow? She should have brought a book. Huh, that would have made him right about grading papers and reading.

She followed a narrow dirt path through the weeds on the dike.

Faye's dad stays to himself. Probably strict. Maybe why she's so quiet, and she just stays out of his way.

She, too, had tried to stay out of the way. How was she to understand all the comings and goings following her father's death. Her aunts and uncles and Pop at the house, the kitchen full of food and people spilling over to the living room and onto the porch. The family and most of the town met at the church. Everyone unsettled, itchy. Finally, outside, the adults chatted, some laughed quietly, and her cousins and she couldn't wait to go home and change. And, the turtle. She'd tried to help a turtle. She moved it from the street to the lawn, then people parked on the lawn.

A shallow dam, down there. Kids below the dam, in the bushes. They're building a raft. Then what? Float to where? Why?

Francis and Kathy were getting counseling. What a concept. Was she too late for it, too many years, too many miles away? Had her life turned out as she'd planned? Did she have a plan? Become a teacher, then what? She was sounding dark, like the little girl on the bus that day. When did youth get extinguished? Dead end, here, already? One semester after the other until one day she would awaken as an overweight old maid with swollen ankles, hair falling out and retired? Perhaps. And, now she really sounded like that girl. "Faye." She said her name. Faye. Yes, her eyes.

She fished in her pocket for a smoke as a silver phalanx of glistening doves appeared and swooped across the grey skies over the river then disappeared in a blink.

They stay here, never leave, many of these kids. Generations of daughters follow their mothers' recipes, sons work in their fathers' trades. Same churches, same Sunday dinners. Everything here for them, in a manageable scale. Why leave? And, newcomers. The college brings them. New businesses move in for the cheap labor, low overhead, affordable housing. Second homes in the country for rich Philly folks who see themselves as hunters and fishermen, outfitted with L.L. Bean's finest and raising local hackles. There's a big distrust here for newcomers and anyone who doesn't work with their hands—for flatlanders.

Francis' father worked with his hands.

Not a great example.

Faye

"May I ask you to stay for just a moment?" Victoria had placed herself at the head of Francis's row in anticipation of the bell. "Just a moment, Faye?"

Faye stared at her then stepped aside. The room emptied in seconds.

"Have we met?" Victoria asked.

"Yes."

"On a bus?"

Faye stared.

"You have had an influence on me, Faye."

Nothing.

"You and Francis—"

"You're kind to Francis, but there's really no one thing you or anyone can do. It will be time and the small, immeasurable things," Faye said.

"I've been in his shoes."

"No, you haven't. If we're going to talk, let's talk about something else."

"Fair enough. I wonder at the why and what-if? In my own life. What if I had stepped off that bus in farm country that day as you suggested? What if I hadn't gone to college and fulfilled my dream to teach? What ever happened next with you? How was your probably amazing life while I was writing papers at college?"

"You've fulfilled your dream? Congratulations."

"Okay, you're right. I'm just getting started."

Green eyes bored into hers. "No rich doctor, right?"

"No. No doctor," Victoria said.

"Now it's a janitor."

Victoria blushed. "I, I'm not sure of that and how would you—?"

"While you were in college, I was in prison."

"Oh my god! Why? I'm so sorry. Faye!"

"How old are you?"

"I'm twenty-four."

"And you think I was in prison."

"Oh."

"I was sent to a special school to learn to be like you."

The bell for the next class rang.

"Faye, I hope you didn't try to become like me. Everyone is unique. Special in their own way."

"No, they're not. I have to go." She slipped away, and Victoria stood alone.

With the Principal

William Howard Hill stood, arms folded with his back to Victoria. He stared out his window, the one that looked out onto the practice field, now beneath a foot of snow. Just a couple months until the team would be back out there. The months without football were insufferable. That junior QB last year—Mazzante—that kid looked promising. They could take the conference with that kid. Big trophy. They engrave the principal's name just below the name of the school.

He sighed and turned to her. "Ms. Merritt, it's the senior class that is responsible for organizing the district's spring play. Traditionally, a classic, traditionally produced by Ruth Walters. You are aware that there are big gaps in your department with Miss Walters and Leroy Samson having been called to duty in Iraq, and may God be with them. That leaves only you and your relatively light schedule in the position to head this year's production.

You'll see some of the past posters rolled up in the library: Wilder, Chekov, Beckett. I suggest that you choose the play rather than exhaust some democratic student process sure to end in a bad choice."

Victoria sat stiffly in front of his desk.

"You'll want to get started immediately, and next month you will have priority use of the auditorium after school four nights a week. You'll have to work around scheduled weekend events. Prior to that, we've contracted with the Mason's for the use of their hall for rehearsals." He turned, unbuttoned his jacket, and spread it, hands on hips. "The play's always sold out. No pressure, though." He showed his teeth.

"Howie, if I may? I would be doing the students, you and the district a great disservice were I to accept your offer. I was not a theater major. I read, I write, I teach and I'm afraid that's about all there is to my life. I've been to numerous plays. I love the theater, but to produce and direct, I'd be lost."

He buttoned his jacket and turned to the window. "Did I say this was an offer? Is that what I said, Victoria? These things sneak up on us, and all-of-a-sudden it's opening night. I suggest you get started."

"But, Howie, I don't know anything about—"

"Lean on Max. He always helps with the sets. He does theater in the summers—theater in Philly—big circle of weirdo thespian friends. Just keep them behind the scenes, and make sure my school—our district—looks good."

"Howie—"

"That will be all, Victoria." He came from behind his desk, crossed to the door and held it open.

Victoria went straight to the loading dock. "Max? Max!"

"Hey, how you doin?" He stepped out from behind a six-foot, shrink-wrapped pallet of paper goods. Come out to see how the other half lives?"

"No, I— Your face!"

"Kidding. What can I do ya for?"

"And, you're limping, Max. What happened?"

"Granny. Little old lady with a purse—"

"A grandmother hit you with her purse?"

"Yeah, right."

"Max, I'm not tracking this."

"Bar across the river, next to the bowling alley. Live music Saturday nights, right? So, I'm havin a couple beers, and Granny sits down next to me. Looks like my old Sunday school teacher. We start chatting, and I buy her a drink, a glass of wine. Merlot. So, we're talkin about how she's alone and fills her days with books, and we're talkin about what she reads, and the band starts playin, and near the end of the first set they play a ballad, and I take Granny out for a little spin. Next thing I know, her World's Strongest Man, idiot grandson and his merry men are putting a new doorway in the place with my head, 'Cause we don't like fuckin strangers tryin to get into Granny's purse!'"

"Max, I'm so sorry. You look terrible."

"Yeah, well, a couple old school biker dudes pulled the merry men off me and left me alone with Junior. He doesn't do so well with a kick in the nuts, and I might have missed one of his ribs. They'll probably be hitting me up for damages—the bar. Fred and Lou, the biker guys, said not to worry about it, they'll vouch for me. Also, Granny's going to need new glasses."

"Max." She touched his cheek.

"Ow. Okay already? What's up? Whatta ya need?"

She stepped back and took a breath. "Howie says you help with the play each year."

"Oh, no. It's you this time?"

"I'm afraid so."

He stepped forward and took her hand in both of his. "Well, congratulations and my deepest condolences." He attempted a smile. "Ouch!" His fingers to his face. "Sorry.

I'll bet you need help and maybe a stiff drink. You're lookin a little green, yourself."

"I'm sure."

"How bad is it? I mean, you ever done this before? Produced a play?"

"No."

"It's bad, then. Howie doesn't like to be embarrassed. Kinda that little man thing."

Francis Conscripted

Victoria had expected pushback from Francis. Of course, he was busy: school, work, Faye, family, counseling. She slid the coffee basket into place, poured fresh water into the little brewer on her desk and pushed the switch. He'd be showing up in a few minutes, and this morning's goal was to win him over as one of the production crew. There he was.

"Hey Ms. M."

"Francis."

He put his books on one of the student desks, opened his jacket and sat at the corner of her desk. "So, s'up today? Got my homework done, Mom checked the spelling, and I think I'm good to go." He reached for a cup.

"Francis, you're aware that we're preparing for a performance. Your sister has volunteered to be the stage manager and has already proven to be invaluable. Quite organized, Kathy."

"Yeah, she claims I'm the clean-freak, but you should see her room." He poured.

"Your classmates joining this production will be gaining an appreciation for the work that goes into a performance and the nearly unimaginable human capital spent making something look natural and easy."

"Yeah, I'll bet. Lotta work, huh?"

"There's more, though. They will see the power of the arts and the animation of the written word."

He took a sip and checked the clock. "Right."

She checked the clock. "I would like you to join us, Francis. To be a part of our production company."

"Ha! No, but thanks. Cripes, I mean..."

Had she called it right, or what? No hesitation. "Francis, this is going to help your grade immeasurably, and in the process, you will have an instrumental role in bringing a Pulitzer Prize-winning play to life in our community."

He set his cup next to the brewer, took another glance at the clock, stood and tidied his books in preparation to leave. "Kinda busy right now: work, school and all."

"Perhaps we can be somewhat flexible around your schedule."

"I don't think so."

She reached across the desk and poured herself a cup. "I'll ask Mr. Hill to speak with someone at the bakery." Another glance at the clock. "You better get going. See you in an hour."

Victoria Shares Thoughts About Max

"No it's just Max, not *June* and Max." The young African American woman leaned on her forearms at Victoria's little breakfast table, a manifest power in her presence. "He's a wonderfully deranged guy who caught my scent, but mine was just the first when he got back from the desert. You have no idea how many he's tracked, since. But, 'Junie Bear' stuck around cause she had no better offers." She pulled a grape from the bunch and— bright teeth—popped it into her mouth.

They were in their Saturday morning pajamas, Victoria and June, Max's friend and theater tech he'd summoned from People's Light and Theater Company in Philly. She'd be spending two nights a week, here, sleeping on Victoria's couch.

"How did you meet?" Victoria asked.

"We crossed paths at the Port Authority. Both damaged. In shock. Trying to find our way home. He was still in uniform, on crutches and headed here. I was drifting, back from Alaska. Undone. Grief." She sat back, hands on her waist and looked out the small window above the sink.

"I'm sorry," Victoria said. She took a sip, "Your grief, is it—?"

"We were talking about Max."

"Of course. Sorry. To tell the truth, I'm a bit drawn to him. More than a bit, actually."

"Why?"

"I'm not sure, and it's uncomfortable. He's so, I don't know, solid—larger than life. He talks freely to me. That has never happened: a guy just talking to me about nothing and everything. A good-looking guy. And, this, whatever it is I'm feeling—his hand on my arm. I don't think he's aware. I hope he isn't. He seems distracted, only partially here."

"Distracted?" June laughed. "He's here, there and everywhere. He drifts somewhere between fact and fiction. Probably why he's so right for the theater."

"But, he seems so practical, capable."

"Max's world. He's still making his way back. Dealing with the terror anyway he can. He saw too much." June pulled another grape. "He's a hero. And, yes, he's attractive and fun and making shit up as he goes, and he may never stop. Just keeps makin it up and movin on. He drank a lot, and we shared our stories and a few tears at that Port Authority bar. He asked me to come with him, help him find his way. I had no plans, so, what the hell? I ended up here—the theater in Philly. He taught me stage operations. I've been doing sets and lights a few years, now. It's taken that long for me to sift through him. Separate what's real from what's not."

"He makes things up? Lies?"

"He knows smart weapons, and he uses them. Another thing and spoiler alert: he doesn't attach." June got up and emptied her cup in the sink. "He'll be here any minute. Okay if I get a quick shower?"

"Of course."

"Hey, hey, my lovelies, is that fresh coffee?"

He smelled like a six-foot micro-brewery with a lingering hint of cigarettes and after-shave. His approach had been silent through the side door, across the front room and into the kitchen where he nearly made it to the table, lightly bounced off the refrigerator, regained his trajectory, spun a chair and straddled it. June braced.

"Top of the morning, ladies. And, what have we here, mimosas, I hope?"

"OJ, Max." June reached over to the table and poured. "And, you're early."

She grabbed a plate, stabbed two sausages, slabbed toast with jam and dropped it in front of him. "Eat."

"Junie Bear, you know a way to a man's heart, and our kids are gonna be healthy little half breeds." He scratched his solid chest.

"Max, may I reacquaint you with my generous host and our producer, Victoria Merritt? She fried those sausages you're scarfing, and she may have made that excellent jam herself."

"Actually, it's from the farmers' market," Victoria said.

They watched in silence as he consumed the meal like a wood-chipper. "Nice, Max, you wolfed your breakfast. Gotta belch?" June said.

"Nah, I'm good." He reached for the coffee pot and poured.

June leaned back on the counter and folded her arms. "I was telling Victoria about your time in service."

"Yeah, well, a guy's gotta do, ya know?"

"Eight years in The Marines. Had you thought of making it a career?" Victoria sat the milk and sugar next to his cup.

"That was the idea." He stirred. "But they wouldn't promote me. Lieutenant kept passing me over. That and they kept rotating me: desert, home, desert, home. Six times. I got em back, though. Got the Silver Star."

Victoria glanced at June. June nodded.

"How? I'm sorry—if you care to say," Victoria said.

"Saved the lieutenants life. I got shot doing it—the bastard—twice in the vest, once in the leg."

"You saved the life of the man who wouldn't promote you?"

"Go figure. Is there more sausage?"

The Auditions

Saturday afternoon, Principal William Howard Hill's polished loafers extended precariously over the brass rail of the balcony above the Masonic Hall ballroom. He slept soundly. Twenty feet below, Victoria, Marge, Max and June sat in a scramble of brown, pressed steel, folding chairs. The audition committee had been through an ordeal, and it showed: Marge slumped, shoes off and scattered at her feet, June straddled her chair and rested her chin on her hands, Max crossed and uncrossed his legs every twenty seconds, and three yellow pencils poked from Victoria's black, unwinding hair like a frustrated Geisha. They listened and took notes as student pairs, one after the other for the past three hours, diluted and flattened the tense dialogue of Tennessee Williams' *Cat on a Hot Tin Roof*:

> MARGARET: Oh, brick...how long does it have to go on...this punishment... haven't I done time

enough...haven't I served my term...can't I apply for a pardon
BRICK: Maggie you are spoiling my liquor...lately your voice always sounds like you have been running upstairs to tell someone that the house was on fire

"That is very good, thank you; very well read. Please make sure your contact information is on the appropriate sheet by the door, and, again, thank you."

Late in the day Anne Marie stepped up and adjusted the mic. She brushed a dark lock aside with the back of her wrist, and if ever there was natural selection, there was never a part so naturally selected for the moisturized, waxed and indomitable Anne Marie Delucci as the part Tennessee Williams had created when he wrote *MARGARET: young, beautiful, wily and—lately—overlooked by her defeated husband, BRICK.* It is an unpredictable and beautiful moment when two perfectly-matched bodies collide and produce an energy, a new life form where previously they had circled in their autonomous orbits: Maggie the Cat, meet Anne Marie. Anne Marie, Maggie the Cat. The fingertips of her left hand floated down the side of her face, her neck, her breast and landed softly on her thigh as she read, "I sometimes suspect that Big Daddy harbors a little unconscious 'lech' fo' me.... Way he always drops his eyes down my body when I'm talkin' to him, drops his eyes to my boobs an' licks his old chops! Ha ha!"

And, Brick. During the final minutes of the auditions, a large, muscular young man was escorted into the Masonic Hall by a small grey-haired woman in a maroon wool cardigan. Paper hands worried the buttons on her sweater as she and the young man stood mute just inside the door in great contrast to the clamorous room as Anne Marie put Margaret through her paces. When Anne Marie was done reading, the woman approached Victoria, whispered something, pointed to the young man by the door and Victoria nodded. Victoria motioned for him to

step forward and read into the microphone. Showing little
expression, he pulled a fold of paper from his back pocket,
unraveled it and found his place. He leaned down to the
mic and the small woman, his English teacher from the
technical school, raised on her toes and they read:

> BRICK: Do it!--fo' God's sake, do it...
> MARGARET: Do what?
> BRICK: Take a lover!
> MARGARET: I can't see a man but you! Even with my
> eyes closed, I just see you! Why don't you get ugly,
> Brick, why don't you please get fat or ugly or
> something so I could stand it?

The little woman turned away for a moment, then
back.

> BRICK: What did you lock the door for?
> MARGARET: To give us a little privacy for a while.
> BRICK: You know better, Maggie.
> MARGARET: No, I don't know better....
> BRICK: Don't make a fool of yourself.

The small English teacher reached up and seized his
shoulder.

> BRICK: Let go!"

His face tightened with rage. He grabbed her wrist,
stretched to his full height, tore her hand from him and
held it suspended.

A long, audible breath escaped him, he shrank an inch
and relaxed. They looked over to Victoria and the panel.

There were nearly seventy high school students and
teachers in the Masonic Hall that late afternoon, and the
room was at a dead stop. Victoria's chair scraped the floor
as she stood, "Thank you. Thank you. That is impressive.

Please leave your contact information. We'll be in touch."
She looked at June.

June raised her eyebrows as if, "So?"

"Cool, very cool. Looks like that's the last pair, finally."
Max leaned out looking across the women. "Wrap it up,
then, go around the block for a drink?"

"Here, here," Marge agreed.

"Do we take Howie, or just turn out the lights, and
leave him up there?" Max said.

"Shame on you." Victoria smiled.

"Damn tempting," he said.

Green Onions

Max held the black padded door to Franco's Lounge as Marge, June and Victoria entered to dancing, laughter and a bumping Cordovox rendition of *Green Onions*, played by—and it was a bit of a shock for Victoria—Anne Marie's father, Big Al Delucchi.

"Looks like Vegas!" Max yelled. "Little Vegas!"

Pink neon glowed from beneath the back of the bar casting hallucinogenic shadows on the low ceiling. From somewhere in the room, black lights got involved and gave a haunted glow to gel-whitened teeth and turned naturally-clear drinks into clouded bitches brew. Full mirrors on three walls took them further through the looking glass as fourth-year college girls showed a lot of leg and got down with the gussied up local boys. The four of them crowded into two spaces at the bar, ordered a round and watched the dancing.

"Wee, ha!" Max nodded. "Howie don't know what he's missing. Look at that big blond just break that boy. Ooo, and now her girlfriend's joining them. They're gonna wear him out."

"This looks like fun, but I am exhausted," Victoria said. She shoved her drink to the back of the bar. "I will see you all tomorrow afternoon, and good night."

"C'mon, stick around," Max said.

"I'm with you Victoria," June said. "See you tomorrow." She waved to Marge as she and Victoria squeezed through the crowd.

Outside, the rain had stopped, the air fresh, crisp and cool, and June said, "It's great you let me crash at your place."

"Are you kidding? You guys are saving me, and I miss you during the week."

They strolled on shimmering, mica-glittered walks beneath nineteenth century street lamps. Four blocks away, a train rolled slowly north along the river.

"I'm leaving," June said.

"What, when?"

"After this play. I'm getting out of the theater, doing something else."

"What?"

"Something else. I don't know."

"Where?"

"I don't know."

"Why?" Victoria asked.

They walked another block. They were at June's car. "So, Brick?" June asked.

"Yes, I hear you."

June opened her door and asked across the roof, "You're going to do it? You're going to cast a black student as Brick?"

"I'm casting that incredible talent as Brick."

"At the risk of your job?"

Take Me to the River

Marge ordered another round as Big Al's amplified, accordion-like pushing and pulling Cordovox bumped and pumped and deep-bass thumped that irresistible intro.

"C'mon, Max!" Marge called, yanking him out to the floor. "Take me to the river!"

She had some moves from back in the day: funky, dirty and a little greasy. And, now she was doing that V thing, pulling her fingers across her eyes and rolling her hips in a gallop. Back to the bar, sweating and a couple buttons undone, she ordered two Silver Bullets. "And, make those doubles!" she called.

They pounded the vodka and were back on the floor as Big Al Delucchi did a damned fine falsetto of Prince's *Kiss*. Hips rocking and fluid, Marge flexed her claws on Max's chest, and now, they locked behind his neck.

"Hey, there and watch out, foxy lady. Slippery slope." He laughed, unlocked her hands and backed away.

That V, staring thing, was back.

The next morning, June tripped the bell above the door as she entered the tiny bakery. Cases were arranged with Italian confections, and a linen corner table offered a variety of roasted brews. The small, white-haired owner came out from the kitchen. She slowed at the sight of the majestic woman at the counter.

"Buongiorno," June greeted her.

"Buongiorno, signorina." From a long-ago port in southern Italy, there remained a girl's innocent smile.

"Your coffee smells great. May I pour a cup? I'm waiting for a friend."

"Si, sei un angelo." She handed her a cup.

"Grazie."

June sat at a delicate table and leafed through the local arts magazine: open artist studios at the Old Factory this weekend, civic chorus doing Handel, Tony Bennett coming to town...

"Hi," Victoria chimed in.

"Sleep well?" June asked.

"Yes. And you?"

"Nope."

"There's a story, here."

"Uh, huh. The Marge and Max story, and this movie is not yet rated."

"No. Really?"

"You didn't hear the phone, did you?" June said.

"No, when?"

"It was after three; the club was closed. They called."

"And?"

"Wanted us to come down and join them for an early breakfast."

"At three?"

"Yep."

"Then what?"

"I told Max to go to hell and laid awake the next few hours. I finally got up, left you the note and took a walk around this part of town. There are some nasty little neighborhoods in the middle of this bucolic Christian splendor. Black families living in worn out, two-story, tarpaper shacks. Cardboard in the windows and their kids' school looks like a meat-packing plant—nothing like your palace on the hill."

"There is greater diversity on this side of the river."

"That's the term you'd choose, 'Greater?'"

"June—"

"Never mind."

Victoria poured a coffee and came back to the table. "Max and Marge, do you think they—?"

"Why not? I guess I hope they did, that I'm free again, for a while. I mean, it sucks for you, though."

Shoulda, Woulda

Victoria sat at her kitchen table with binders stacked open and her laptop lit. She had trouble concentrating on preparations for Monday's classes. There would be the junior-seniors in the morning and, after lunch, the senior honors, and, well, she'd winged it on Friday and didn't want to let that happen again. She didn't do that great on her feet, and she knew that at least the honors students saw right through her. The play had become all-consuming.

What was she doing? Her job, her classes, the play? How did others do it, her predecessors? Would there come a time in life when things were simple, and one could expect the expected? And, now Max? Should she have said something, to Marge—to Max? Should she have acted? And now he'd slipped away?

Cat on a Hot Tin Roof

"Hey, there, Francis. Shut the door, and put that headset on. We're going to rock and roll, dude." Max cleared a chair next to him at the control deck. In the Martian light, Francis closed the door behind him.

"Look at all those switches. This place is cool."

"Damn straight, it's cool. We have all the fun up here, my man, amazing the audience with special effects, conjuring weird noises and keeping the stage lit so the actors don't bump into each other. Want some chips?" Max passed the bag. "Sea salt and vinegar."

His mouth full, Francis sat down and reached for the headset.

"Whoa, there, pal. Wipe your hands, first."

"Sorry."

"We take care of the weapons, and the weapons take care of us. Semper Fi." Max held out his fist. Francis pounded it and thought, cool guy.

"So, Francis, it's going to be you and me and a couple others up here in mission control throwing switches and pulling strings. But, first we gotta read the script about a hundred times. The director—that'd be her down there on the stage in the mangled hair, nervous sweat and biting her nails—she tells us what she's looking for, and we create it. We get our cues, we mark em in the script, we program these high-tech toys and do whatever we have to do manually each night—which is most of it. We also watch and wait for the shit to hit the fan, and it sure as hell will. Then, we deal with it. Adapt, and overcome, baby. Semper Fi."

Francis pounded it.

"There. Now, flip that toggle and you're live. Say hi to Junie Bear back stage. You still there, my brown sugar sticky buns?"

"Must we, Max?" June's tired voice appeared in Francis' headset.

"Max!" It was Ms. Merritt he heard next. She pointed up to the booth from the stage, "Please?"

"Just catching Francis here up to speed, kids. See, Francis? We're all wired. Sweet Margie's out there, somewhere."

"Top of the booth, Max. Follow spot. Hi, Francis." Ms. Sweeney's voice. "And, we each have a student with us, Max, so try to keep it under wraps, okay?"

"Roger that. And, Margie, first the spot is aimed. *Then*, it comes on, right?"

"Of course."

"Thank you all, crew and cast," Victoria said from the stage. Anne Marie, a word in the wings, please? It will take just a moment. That was nearly flawless, crew, and Max, the light in the closing scene is beautiful."

"Yeah, as long as we avoid the moon drop, Margie. Aim, *then* on," Max said.

"We're getting there, Max; one step at a time," Marge said.

"Have a great night, all. You can go ahead and shut things down, Max, and thank you," Victoria said.

"So, Francis, you have some reading to do—hundred

times. We read it until we know every line, every move," Max said.

"Roger, that." Francis smiled, took off his headset and laid it carefully on the shelf. "Thanks. This is huge."

"We're conjurers, my man. Victory, tragedy, the damned and the dead. And the coolest part? Nothing's real."

"Faye says there'll be trouble opening night."

"Who's Faye? What kind of trouble?"

"My girl. She said rednecks because of Charles and our play."

"When it hits the fan, we deal, right?"

"Right."

"Semper Fi."

For the last time that night, Francis pounded it.

In bed by the dim light of the little porcelain lamp, Francis read Tennessee Williams' notes for the designer:

...there was a quality of tender light on weathered wood, such as porch furniture made of bamboo and wicker, exposed to tropical suns and tropical rains, which came to mind when I thought about the set for this play, bringing to mind also the grace and comfort of light, the reassurance it gives, on a late and fair afternoon in summer, the way that no matter what, even dread of death, is gently touched and soothed by it. For the set is a background for a play that deals with human extremities of emotion, and it needs that softness behind it.

A little over an hour later, he closed the play, crossed the room and turned off the light. The last lines repeating in his head took him off to sleep:

"What you need is someone to – take hold of you—gently, with love and hand your life back to you, like something gold you let go of..."

Howie Takes Charge

In the dark lobby, Principal William Howard Hill slipped his master key into a steel lock and quietly cracked one of the eight fire doors at the back of the auditorium. It hit him like a shovel. The rumor, down there on the stage, was confirmed: Victoria Merritt had chosen a large black student from the technical school to play Brick! Was she? Yes, she obviously was. She was out of her God-forsaken Jewish mind! This was trouble from the start, and he should have seen it coming. He'd hired an outsider, someone not of the valley. He'd assumed she'd get into stride, find the cadence of his school. She obviously hadn't. *Cat on a Hot Tin Roof!* And, he'd let Marge and some of the others talk him into it? Didn't the title say it all? The South? The drinking? The sexual-something innuendoes? What in the hell was he supposed to do with this? This wasn't Harrisburg or New York. This was America, goddam it!

Ben Gazzara, Jack Lord, Paul Newman. Those guys were Brick. What if Paul Newman walked in here right now and saw this? In this school, and Mr. Paul Newman walked in and saw what he saw this very moment? Cool Hand Luke walks into his school and gets slapped right in the face. Oh, Mister Butch Cassidy? Please meet William Howard Hill, principal. He's responsible for the greater-than-thou ethnic woman directing the play in which you so masterfully played Brick. She chose a large, black, football player who lives miles from the nearest bus stop and attends the technical school—The technical school!—to play your part. And, yes, you're right, Mr. Newman, at the end of the day, it all lands in my lap. My wife and I love your movies, by-the-way, and that salad dressing.

William Howard Hill pressed Victoria's room number into his phone and waited.
"Yes? This is Victoria."
"Ms. Merritt, would you please come down to my office during your planning period? Third period?"
"Of course, Howie. Should I bring something? Prepare?"
"No, I'd just like a word."
"Of course."

She sat at her desk scanning the rehearsal schedule and the cast and crew rosters. They'd come a long way in just five weeks. It had been divine to finally move rehearsals from Masonic Hall to the school stage, and things were starting to come together. The adult mentors were taking less responsibility at each rehearsal, and the kids would soon be running things themselves. They weren't there, yet, but at this rate, they may just pull off something great—something far beyond student production status. Anne Marie. Who would have guessed? Of course, the sauterne, the sultry—but the memory? She had read her lines just a couple times and had them down.

She did have to keep an eye on her wardrobe, though. The girl was far too comfortable undressed in public.

And, Charles, dear Charles. They were going to see him on Broadway and on screen, one day. Brick breathed in him, and, beneath his tense restraint, Charles choked back their shared rage. The kids were finding themselves in literature and the arts: Francis at Max's elbow, learning the craft, shadowing a nearly-complete role model—his sister, Kathy, taking charge as stage manager. The phone.

"Yes? This is—"

"You're on your way?"

"Sorry, Howie. Yes, I'm just leaving."

The women in the office looked up when she entered—all three. "Howie asked me to come in."

The receptionist pointed to Howie's closed door. "Uh-huh."

He stood with his back to her, looking out to the practice field. "Please close the door, Victoria, and have a seat, anywhere."

"Hello, Howie." She sat in one of the two leather barrel chairs in front of his desk.

He turned from the window, placed his hands on the back of his chair, showed his teeth and asked, "How's the play coming along?"

This is it, Waterloo, she thought. "I am amazed how well things have come together. I couldn't have asked for more. Your suggestion about Max and his theater connections has made all the difference. And, Marge has been so generous with her time. The kids have really taken to the project. They're taking ownership. It's great to—"

"The lead roles? Anne Marie as Margaret, Maggie. The cat on the tin roof? How's she doing?" He turned back to the window.

Stay on your horse. "Anne Marie is one of the success stories, Howie. For a girl otherwise disengaged from school, she has found herself. Did you know she has a nearly photographic—"

"And, Brick?"

She sat straighter. He continued.

"Brick. Who plays Brick, Margaret's husband, the still handsome and fit former athlete, the favorite son of Big Daddy, the patriarch, the southern white plantation owner? Who plays his son? Someone from the other school, I hear?"

"Yes. Charles Morehouse plays Brick."

"Unusual name, Morehouse."

"We are so fortunate to have Charles and Anne Marie; their chemistry is perfect."

"Their chemistry?" he asked. "There's something between them? Anne Marie and this other student?"

"Charles. Charles Morehouse. Yes, and it's a perfect something. They each have such strength; Anne Marie wears hers on her sleeve. She puts it out there with confidence, commitment, despite what may happen next. She, not unlike Margaret, 'plays it like it lays,' as Max says."

"Max says that?" He looked back over his shoulder. "Anne Marie 'puts out and plays it as it lays?'" A flush rose from his collar.

She pulled hard on the reins and came about. "I am sorry, Howie. Margaret—in the play—she is steadfastly strong in the face of nearly insurmountable difficulty. Anne Marie plays the part wonderfully."

"And, this, this, Brick?" He turned back to the window.

There it is, the shot. She was hit and fully off her horse. She stood bleeding, hands limp at her sides. "What is this about?"

"Please, have a seat, Ms. Merritt." He faced her, came around his chair and sat. His hands on his desk—his praying hands—pointed at her. "You have created a situation, here, with some bad choices. Adjustments must be made, corrections."

"Howie, I don't understand."

"Ms. Merritt. The play you chose is inappropriate. I gave you guidelines which you ignored. You enlisted a team of supporters to assuage my resistance and went on your merry way. Then, from a field of hundreds of qualified and eager students you chose the most under-achieving and nearly-criminal representative of our school to parade half-naked in front of our ninth graders and their parents, the dedicated faculty, district administrators, the superintendent and the mayor. Did I mention that the mayor always attends? And, the spleen-picking, shit-on-a-cracker media?!" There was sweat on his forehead. He was very red.

Over his shoulder, a flock of silver birds climbed the gray sky. They swooped, dove, circled, flipped on their sides and arced as one up and out of the window's frame.

She took a deep breath and let it out. Her horse had run off, stopped, looked back at her and stood steaming at the tree line. She fingered the hilt of her sword. "Howie. Mr. Hill. This isn't about the play or Anne Marie. Shall we address the issue squarely?"

"You want squarely, Ms. Merritt? Two weeks. You have two weeks to repair the damage you've done. Make the proper adjustments, find better actors, clean up their lines and let's have a happy ending."

She drew her sword and advanced. "Brick is black."

"I beg your pardon?"

"Charles, the student playing Brick, he's African American."

He slapped both hands flat on his desk, sprung from his chair and shot his arms out crucified. "No shit!" He paced. "The son of a dying white Mississippi Delta plantation owner, surrounded by his long-suffering white family and his favorite son, the star athlete of his high school and the heart throb of a fifty-five-mile radius, is *black*? That's what this play is about? That's what you have decided this play is about? Low and behold, the heir of Big Daddy's fortune and his wife, his *white* wife—and oh my, doesn't this get better every minute—is what this play is about? That's what you want to stuff up the nose of this community?" He was back at the window, his back to her, arms folded.

Incredible. Does he hear himself? "Howie, Mr. Hill, can we look at this from another position? Can we make this not about race?"

Quiet and calm, "I haven't chosen to, you have," he said to the window.

"Anne Marie and Charles bring honesty and believability to their roles that supersedes their personal lives. Whatever, whoever they are off stage, reappears as Brick and Margaret under the lights."

"He's black. That doesn't go away."

"Is that what you see when you see Brick, when you hear him, see his struggle with himself, with his family, with Margaret—the actor's skin tone? He is Brick."

"It's what the entire audience will see."

She sheathed her sword and sat. "With all respect, would you be more convincing?" she asked.

He looked back over his shoulder. "What are you talking about?"

"If you were to play Brick? You're white. Would that be believable?"

"I don't—"

"Brick is repelled by his beautiful, seductive wife. Brick is an alcoholic and has a past in question, perhaps a homosexual liaison. Would you be a fit for Brick? Would I? Would Max or Marge? Would Coach? Well, maybe Coach. Charles Morehouse begins his acting career here, on this stage, at your school. He has a rare gift that will take him far, and you are giving him his start. There will likely come a time—a Hollywood awards ceremony—when your name will be included in those he thanks."

He turned, opened his jacket and landed hands on hips, "Nice try, but no cigar. Make some changes, fast, or there'll be a burning hole where you sit."

Half-day of School and That Friday Afternoon

Francis balanced two bales of straw on a wheelbarrow, and, glancing toward the bike shed every few seconds, moved the bales across the dirt. Faye had filled the spouted watering can at the hose by the paint booth and leaned for ballast, the dogs close at her heels as she met Francis back at the coop. Faye enjoyed helping with the pigeons. Francis wasn't all that comfortable around the Sebastians.

"It's okay, Francis. Really. They like you, in their own way."

"You say."

Lou was in the bike shed on his haunches spitting explosive, single-syllabled epithets as he tried to fit a new carburetor on the FXR, and Fred was giving a haircut to one of their buddies in the outdoor barber chair across the yard. The bearded guy in the chair, a flowered bed sheet gathered at his neck, had hard-time tattoos similar to

Fred's but spent a lot longer in the all-you-can-eat line. Francis overheard their musings:

"So, what the hell's happenin with the oil? Three bucks a gallon one day, five bucks the next."

"The Arabs control the pricing," Fred said, comb in one hand, scissors at work in the other.

"Where the hell's it all come from?"

"What?" Fred pushed his friend's head forward and continued clipping.

"The fuckin oil."

"Well, they pump it outta the ground."

"A goddam idiot knows that! I mean, they keep pumpin it out, but nobody's pumpin it back in, far as I can tell. So, where's it all come from?"

"They say it was dinosaurs fell into the swamp, got stomped down and turned to oil."

"Musta been a helluva lot of them sonsabitches."

The six-days-a-week gospel radio in the work bay gave up the ghost to bluegrass on Friday afternoons. The coop's squeaking door hinges and pigeon chatter were counterpoint to Ralph Stanley's high-pitched and haunted *Man of Constant Sorrow*. Faye flushed the birds from their perches and got to work. Rubber gloves, she pulled out much of the old straw from the cubbies. Francis raked out the floor, placed fresh straw in the nests, pulled the feed trays from their hooks and took them outside. He flushed them with the hose, wiped them out, hung them back in place and filled them with fresh grain. Faye employed similar labor for the water bottles.

Inside the coop, Francis kept his voice low and told her he'd be scarce for the next couple weekends, that the rehearsals were getting intense; the opening was in two-and-a-half weeks. She wondered how it was going, said she saw a proof of the program in art class and it looked pretty cool with Big Daddy on the cover, his hand balled in a fist. She said that, as funny as it seemed, she'd invited Fred and Lou and a few of their friends to the play.

He asked why.

She said she wasn't sure, but she had a feeling. She asked was Ms. M calming down some?

He said it was all coming together, that when everything was working right—the actors knowing their lines well enough to say them the way people really talked and move about the stage the way people really moved, and when the lighting and sound were on time and just right—well, it was friggin magic.

Meanwhile, the birds rested on the power lines above and awaited the tin cup signal.

That Friday Night

The screen door rattled. "Hey, you in there. Open up." The front room was lit by the solo table lamp next to Victoria's ancient and over-stuffed chair. From the porch, June stared into the lonely silence of an Edward Hopper painting. Victoria closed the script, went to the door and flipped the hook.

"Am I glad to see you. How was the drive?"

"Dark. There are some lonely roads in this state at night. Long week?" June dropped her backpack by the door.

"It shows?"

June was at the refrigerator. "You got beer, thanks. Want one?" She grabbed two. "So." She handed one to Victoria and dropped into the sofa. "The shit hit the fan?"

"That brings it into focus."

"Just a matter of time. How bad?"

"He said unless I make some big changes, there's going to be, 'a burning hole where I sit.'"

"Howie?"

"Yes."

"So, you went to the superintendent?"

"They're of the same mind."

June took a swig and raised her bottle. "Whoo-eee, and welcome back to 1960!"

"This must really make you angry," Victoria said.

"Why? You're the one getting fired."

"But, you're black."

"Oh, right."

"June, how can you make fun of this?"

"Because it's a fucking joke, Victoria." She leaned forward. "The world has passed those two Neanderthals by. They're stuck here in the dark, mouth breathing and picking fleas off each other's butts. A bastion of 'keeping my life the way it was when I was a kid' and everything all Cheez Whiz and *Petticoat Junction*. Thank God someone like you comes along and breaks the lock so the kids can escape."

"Do you think they'll fire me?"

"Hell, yes! First year teacher, stirring up the waters with her bad choices and big city ways? Honey, you're screwed."

"Thank you. I'll sleep better, now." Victoria took a hit on the beer.

"Well, you're screwed unless you make Howie's changes, and it's a little late for that."

"How could I make the changes? And, that's really not the question. It's *why* would I? Think of the moral damage. I can't replace Charles. I won't replace Charles, and they'll fire me, and I have no back-up plan." She sat the bottle on the table, went to the kitchen, brought back a box of hard pretzels, handed it to June, snagged the beer from the table and paced.

"Thanks. You don't stand a chance unless—"

"What?" Victoria turned and headed back across the room.

"Unless you fight this."

Victoria stopped, "There's no way, June. The superintendent is with Howie."

June rose from the sofa, shifted her weight, chin up and hand on her hip, "Let me *ax* you, girl, do the word 'media' ring a bell?" She crunched a chunk of pretzel in strong teeth.

Victoria sat. "Are you saying tell on Howie? Tell the press he's racist?"

June relaxed her stance and swallowed. "Hmmm, I hadn't thought of something so direct, but that's interesting."

"My first year and I'm destroying it—all of it: my teaching, finding a guy and I'll never work again. How can they do this, be so closed off, so sure of themselves?"

"Gotta watch that *they* shit. Lumping everyone together; that's a big part of the problem."

"I didn't mean—"

"Some things are bigger than us. Maybe situations we find ourselves in we didn't plan on, aren't ready for and don't know what the hell to do with. But, we can't just quit. Max got shot in Iraq. He sure as hell didn't plan on that. You thought LBJ put this whole thing to bed, right? You thought Martin had won? Tell you what, sweetheart, racism morphs, then it morphs again, and the rich get rich and the poor get screwed."

Victoria let out a long breath, stood and walked over to the screen. "Uh-huh." The door creaked and slammed as she stepped onto the porch.

"You running away, or you want company?" June asked through the screen.

Quiet, crickets and the occasional passing car.

"Both sound good."

"I can only do one, honey. I ain't runnin." June went out. Just ten feet away, through the neighbor's window, they were watching Friday night boxing.

Victoria's cigarette flared, faded, and she exhaled. "Do I give them the satisfaction of firing me, or do I quit and let them force me out?"

"That's it? Those are the options? Strong, smart, white chic's just gonna fold?"

"What would you do?"

"I'd pick up a stick."

The Word "Media" Rings a Bell

They sat in a corner of the little Italian bakery and sipped from foamy cups: June, Victoria and Melanie Korn, the *City Arts and Society* columnist from *The Gazette*.

"How do you know syndicated columnist extraordinaire Pete Baxter, champion of the oppressed, slayer of city councils? I'm so sorry. Has it been painful?" the reporter asked. She grinned. "Hearing that name takes me back."

"It was a few years ago," June said.

"Sweet guy, among friends, but get his hackles up and you're going down," Melanie said. She glanced down and fastened a button over escaping belly freckles. "We worked together at the paper in Palm Beach for a short time, back in the day. A time when we thought our columns helped advance the human condition; when newsrooms looked less like insurance offices. So, how do you know him?"

June finished her cup. "We were close in San Francisco. I baked him cookies. It was another life." She rapped the table once. "But, the reason we called is Victoria here is facing a dilemma at the school. One that's—" She looked at Victoria. "One that's morally critical, and, professionally speaking, life and death. She's staring down racism."

"You have my attention."

June patted Victoria's hand, "Go for it, girl."

Victoria unrolled the situation for Melanie. Melanie pushed back from the table, checked the straining button and locked her fingers behind wild, red hair. "I can see where this is an attack-worthy issue, but, maybe for op-ed, maybe a letter to the editor. My job here is to praise Caesar."

"Uh-huh," June said. "And, Caesar, so to speak, would be the mayor of this segregated fairyland?"

"Hah! No, but try that on her when you see her at your opening. She'll tear you a new one."

"We were wondering if you would want to preview the play while we're still in rehearsal," Victoria said.

"And?" Melanie asked.

"We'll hope for the best. We would be honored if you were to see what we're doing, what these kids are doing."

"It's the real deal," June said.

Melanie had never been to the school on the hill. In her six months at *The Gazette*, this may be just the second time she'd been on this side of the river. She pulled in beneath the buzzing lights of the parking lot. She was beginning to feel the old juices again, her blood warmer tonight than yesterday. The visit to this school and covering this play actually had some moral meat to it. *First Year Teacher Changes District's Tone.* Hah!

The banks of double doors to the dark lobby were locked. Of course. How the hell do you get into this Tupperware fortress? She edged around to the back of the school. There, lit by a caged security light, a single steel door propped open. A crack in the parapet. She entered the dark backstage to resonant, southern voices:

"Big Daddy, I will not allow you to talk that way, not even on your birthday, I—"

"I'll talk like I want to on my birthday, Ida, or any other goddam day of the year and anybody here that don't like it knows what they can do!"

"You don't mean that!"

Melanie felt her way behind the set, stooping beneath ropes and stepping over diagonal wooden braces. Already she could tell the acting was a notch above what she'd expected—the voices authentic, the timing believable. Her eyes were adjusting as the rehearsal continued just a few feet away on the other side of the flats.

"What makes you think I don't mean it?"

"I just know you don't mean it."

"You don't know a goddam thing and you never did!"

She was near the darkened wings and rounded what must look like the corner of a room from the audience side. Low moaning and "shhh's" came from just ahead. Oh shit, she thought, as their shadows came into subdued view. That would be a blowjob.

Out on the stage, the production continued.

"Big Daddy, you don't mean that."

"Oh, yes, I do, oh, yes, I do, I mean it! I put up with a whole lot of crap around here because I thought I was dying."

There, backstage in the near dark, was a big silhouette of a guy sitting on the edge of a chair, his head back. On her knees, between his bare extended thighs, her collection of bracelets rattled lightly with her head's hydraulic pulse.

Damn. She probably shouldn't be seeing this, though it was wonderfully entertaining. Melanie backed a few steps into deeper shadow.

"Brick! Hey Brick!"

The big silhouette jerked to his feet and yanked pajama bottoms up. His local service provider was knocked to her butt, rebounded like a cheerleader, handed the big guy a crutch and they disappeared into the raking lights.

"I didn't call you, Maggie. I called Brick."

Okay. She hadn't seen this. No way did she see this, as she followed dim light to the opposite stage wing. She'd wait for a break in the action, then make her sweet and dear-me-ignorant entrance.

Two days later, Victoria handed the draft back to Melanie. "You like it!"

"Quite impressive." Melanie lowered her latte leaving a foamy moustache. "We'll be back tonight for some photos, then the article hits the front page of the entertainment section Thursday. As you see, both your principal and the superintendent claim responsibility for a 'loosening of the shackles.' That line was brilliant on my part, and I wish my editor hadn't cut it. Instead, it comes out as '...the casting genius of this ground-breaking production.'"

"Thank you," Victoria said.

"Hey, don't thank me. I wouldn't have written it if it wasn't so. Quite a production, quite a story. Want to hear another one? Hard headed woman and a soft-hearted man? The one where the plot thickens?"

"What? Which story?"

"The one where your ass is still in the fire?"

Victoria scratched the back of her neck and dropped her hands into her lap, "Okay?"

Francis is Late

The little blue Toyota was coming in hot. It rattled the glass at the guard shack, slowed slightly past the inert row of cars in the employee lot and scratched sideways to a stop. There was a grinding of small gears and the Corolla lurched, corrected, grinded, lurched and backed into space #137. The guard's golf cart, it's blue light flashing, pulled to a rest in front of the car as Francis stepped out.

"With your girlfriend again, ain't?" the guard said.

"Yeah. Sorry. Time just slips away from us."

"You gotta stop at the guard shack before proceeding to the company lot. I gotta check you off—check you off on the clipboard. You oughta know that, now that I'm tellin ya a third time."

Francis hot-footed it toward the packaging and shipping entrance, the golf cart and its flashing blue light rolled next to him. "Yeah, sorry. Won't happen again. Once the play's over, then it'll be better—my schedule."

"I gotta go back to the guard shack now and check you off—number 137—and after the fact. Try to figure out what the hell time you actually entered the facility and then mark it off on the goddam clipboard and it's makin my job butt-fuckin painful is what it is."

"Thanks, I appreciate it." Francis opened the heavy steel door and entered the bakery.

Victoria Falls

They sat on Victoria's side porch in the late afternoon. "How old's that Margaret, by the way? Musta been held back a couple grades, right?" Max asked.

"I beg your pardon?" Victoria asked.

"That feline actress chick, plays Margaret? Mary Ann something? Looks like thirty, acts like forty?"

"Anne Marie. She is a junior and nineteen, soon twenty. She had a slow start. Why?"

"Stuff happening, there. You might want to keep an eye on it."

"What, Max?"

"Just sayin. Her, Charles and the ol horizontal bop, is all."

"I am aware, thank you. But, what they do as individuals—"

"Not on school property, it isn't. Be your ass in a sling if they do, and they may damn well have already."

"I've taken precautions, thank you."

"You think they have? They've taken precautions? I'm counting the months, here."

They won't find themselves alone again."

"Hell, I mean, they drive, right? Go parking. Do it in a car."

"Charles doesn't have a car."

"That girl does. Drives a hot rod. Get it?"

"Anne Marie."

"Whatever. Ya know, Vic, it's nice sittin here and chattin with you. You want another beer?"

"Victoria, Max. I'm Victoria."

He grabbed her half-empty and was into the refrigerator, the screen door pop, pop slammed, and he was seated again.

"We've never actually spent time alone. I mean, this is nice. At first, I had you pegged for an oddball English teacher with your head so buried in books you hardly noticed you had your period. But you got style and guts. And, when you're relaxed like this, not wound so tight, hair fallin outta your ponytail, and your shorts showin some good leg, you look different. I mean, pretty— attractive. I mean you always do, and look at you blush. You kinda like me, too, don't you?"

"Mind if I smoke?" she asked. Victoria tapped one from the pack, lit up, stood and went over to the edge of the porch. She sat on the top step with her back to him. She took a long drag and stabbed out the cigarette on the base of the porch pole. "Yes, Max, I like you. And, thinking out loud, maybe I'll figure out why."

She glanced down and swatted her ankle.

"It's surely not that you occasionally turn up the volume and go off grid with your drinking and fighting. There are other ways to resolve things, you know, and I think having given those a chance you might prefer them. There's something going on between heart and hand with you. June told me how you brought her up in the business, took her under your wing when she needed a warm place just as much as you. As combative as you can be, you like people. You're a caretaker. That incident at the lounge with the elderly woman—you were being nice. You are sensitive with Francis, and he looks up to you.

You've helped me beyond words. You have initiative, you're smart and quick to action. And, I've given this some thought: that night with Marge was just circumstance, the perfect storm for her. For you, just another squall."

"Nothing happened, remember?"

"You've both testified, and the jury's out.

So, why do I like you? What do I find attractive? The caretaker part for sure. Your awareness and that you form decisions quickly, and you are engaged in—comfortable in—the practical world. That you are spontaneous, and I never know what you'll bring up next. That you are open and for the most part non-judgmental." She turned toward him. "And, you've heard it here, you're physical—a bit of a hunk."

He leaned back, crossed a leg, hands behind his head like he was beginning to enjoy this and wanted more. It was not forthcoming. He sat forward, elbows on knees. "I gotta leave."

"What?"

"The school, this town—I have to leave come summer."

"But, you'll be here next year."

"No, Vic. I'm leaving, for good."

"But, your job."

"This is okay, like, for a day job, but June's leaving the theater, leaving the state. Tired of the cars, the crowds, 'the plastic carbonated crap,' she says, and getting back to nature."

"She mentioned she was leaving. And, you're going with her?"

"No. She was my main man at the theater when I wasn't there. Now that she's leaving, I have to go back full time."

"This is your job, Max." Your school, my—

"It's just a job, Vic. I gotta be there for them, the company. My heart's in it."

No. What is he doing? "Max, you do so well here. The faculty, the students, everyone loves you."

"Thanks. I try, and I'll miss everyone."

Victoria stood on empty legs and wrapped one arm around the porch pole, her back to him. "I feel as though we're just at the beginning."

"Vic—"

"You're right. I'm sorry. I'm wishing instead of thinking. Of course, you have your life. You have to do what's right, for you—your passion."

"One of them," he said.

"You follow your heart." She heard him rise behind her. He took two steps. His thumb brushed her neck as his hand lighted on her shoulder, and a power switch flipped in her belly.

"So, we gettin down, or what?"

She turned and stared at him—his eyes, the wrinkles at the corners, and she watched his slow grin arrive from across the bridge.

"Buy me dinner, then we'll see."

What Would You Make Liberace for Breakfast?

The sun slipped over the crests of eastern summits, skimmed the tree tops on the islands just off the lumberyard and, low and red, warmed a long raspberry patch on the northern shore of the Susquehanna River. The slow current flowed deep, cutting away the bank beneath weeping branches where avian shadows competed in song. Just downriver, the arched bridge hummed every now and again as the lights of early commuters fanned the steel grid surface.

Arm-in-arm, her head against his shoulder, they strolled upstream at the water's edge. He held her hand as they climbed the bank over a washout and sat in the short grass, their shoes mid-air a foot above the current. Two young people: one blonde and one dark, one square and solid, the other curved and soft. Neither had slept, and they hadn't noticed. Max released a long breath, slid his hands behind him and leaned back. Victoria stretched out and laid her head in his lap. Strings of crimson clouds in the East moved as a unit at what must have been a hundred miles an hour, and to the west the heavens were a dark ultramarine, those clouds platinum smoke. He watched the slow ripple of the water, the insects hovering at the surface and the occasional white flip close to shore.

"You probably think I'm strong and crude."

It was one of those Max moments: barging in up to speed from who knew where, and it would take her a few moments to catch up. She waited. Give him time.

"You'd be half right."

A few more commuters crossed the bridge, most from south to north, to work in the stores and mills, some at the college.

"I'm pretty vulnerable these days, not so strong, I guess. I just sugar-coat it in crude."

Did he want her to smile? She glanced up. His stare stayed on the water.

"Kinda different for me, being around you, watching you this year. I felt like we were in an orphanage or something, and you were new here, and neither of us had anyone, and I felt a connection with this odd new kid, like it made sparks, and there was this animal energy, and I wondered if you felt it, too."

Her eyes wider, she fought her urges. Give him his time.

"I *am* an orphan—since I was five—then a couple times a foster kid. So, the military gives me a family, a home. Eight years later that goes south, and I keep busy keepin it simple and doing the things I love like the theater and other things to pay the rent, like custodian. Then, I'm going about my business doing the pay the rent things, and this fresh wind blows up the front steps, and, like, she's smart and pretty, and I think she really cares about the kids, and she carries herself like she really means it."

He'd be feeling her tears in his lap any second.

"So, I start looking for chances to talk to her about anything. Stupid stuff like mops and light bulbs, I guess, and then, looking back after the fact, I'm thinking she's gotta think I'm pretty crude. Not her style. Then the play comes along and I'm all, 'Holy shit, this puts us in the same room together every day for weeks!'"

She swallowed hard. She hadn't moved.

"Then we're actually in it together and being friends and then dinner last night, and all, and now I'm thinking everything's changed for sure, but how?"

...and all...? *And all?* She had to say something—to say that 'and all' meant something. She rustled into sitting next to him. He pulled his knees in and sat up.

"Max, I think I'm falling in love with you."

He stood and helped her to her feet. He pulled her close and hugged her. "Crazy, huh?" He stood back, smiled big, took her hand and started back the trail toward the truck. "What say we get some breakfast?"

She walked just a half step behind. He said, *Crazy, huh?* What did that mean? Her heart beat much faster than her steps, her eyes bounced between the back of his neck and the trail.

"Max, do you sometimes make things up as you go? Little untruths?"

They were back to the narrow stream that cut through the path. She had barely made it across on their way out. He let go of her hand, easily leaped across and continued on. She hesitated, took a breath and surprised herself at making it again. She caught up to him.

"Do I lie?" he said, not looking back.

"That would be an indelicate way to ask," she said. Minutes passed, and she could feel him thinking. They were back at the truck. He opened her door and held it as she slipped in.

"No." He closed the door.

They had dined at an Italian restaurant up the pike and had window seats overlooking the valley. The sunset, the lights far below and the candlelight she'd remember years later; she hardly tasted her food. In him, she accepted she was beautiful.

They had stayed past midnight, the chairs stacked on tables around them, and the staff wanted to go home. He left a hundred-dollar tip, and they crossed an empty lot to his truck. He opened her door, came around the front and slid in behind the wheel. They sat and drifted out of orbit.

"Liberace? No way."

"As sure as I sit here."

"So, he really spent the night?"

"He did."

"And, you guys made him breakfast? What would you make Liberace for breakfast? I mean, you guys just happened to have some caviar in the back of your fridge?"

"We had tea, toast and mom's homemade jam; better than anything he had ever tasted."

"Well, I can't top that. I met Bob Hope, once; shook his hand, at least. He visited the troops. Your mom still around?"

"Yes, in the same little apartment in Harrisburg."

"You see her much?"

"When I can. It's been a busy year."

"How's she doing, I mean, with you gone and all?"

"I think she's happy. She's met someone. They attend readings, concerts. They go to church together. He's retired from teaching, a nice man."

He started the truck and pulled out of the lot. "Maybe I'll get to meet em, sometime."

Her wheels left the ground.

At his place—a deserted stone farmhouse—in his bed, she feigned calm and confidence, like they'd done this often. In fact, she was near panic, her first time in love. But he was caring, and they began slowly, nothing like she'd imagined.

Afterward, she wanted a smoke and wrapped the sheet around her and went down to the kitchen, came back and watched him in the shower. When it was her turn, she closed the door.

At four-thirty, they drove through the sleeping neighborhoods, over the bridge and down into the river park. They followed the moonlit trail through the woods to its end, made their way to the water's edge and continued upstream as a new day appeared from behind the mountains.

Opening Night

Victoria entered the dark set and moved to downstage center. So quiet, here, she thought, this transformative space in suspension for as long as the curtain remains between the audience and us. Her hand trembled as she reached to the split in the curtain.

"Uh-uh." It was Max in her headset. "Go to stage right. You can check the crowd from there."

"Thanks, Max." From the wing, she peeked beyond the proscenium, and there they were: five hundred people buzzed and fussed with jackets and purses, scanned their programs and awaited the curtain. Along the back wall of the auditorium, standing-room-only was a leaning line of somewhat under dressed young men and women, most in truckers' caps. To call them "country" would have been generous. Howie had said it, "sold out," and it was. No surprise, there. However, there were faces in the house lights she hadn't expected: dark faces in this white community, and they must have arrived early; the seating was on a first-come basis. The broad, sixth row center was men and women rarely seen on this side of the river.

Behind them, too, in the seventh row were unexpected patrons. Faye was there, the jewel in the crown anchored left and right by three and two exceptionally large, mature, tattooed white men with their arms crossed. Three wore kerchief headbands. Those WZXR Buffalo Springfield, *For What It's Worth* lyrics came to her. She tried not to dwell as she turned and walked onto the set.

"You online, my man?" Max's voice woke Francis' headphones.

"Roger, that."

"Okay, pal, this is for all the marbles."

"Got it, Max. Control booth is locked and loaded."

"Slow dim to seven, and bring up the overture."

"Roger." Rose Mary Clooney's *Come On-A My House* came through the walls as from an AM radio in the next room promising apples and plumbs and apricots, too.

"Semper Fi."

"Semper Fi."

"I'm backstage with your teacher, our ever-lovely producer and director, all night, unless someone needs me somewhere else."

"Max (muffle, static, shuffle), please!" Victoria's voice.

"Yes, Max, stick it in a vice!" June's voice.

"Roger, Junie. You guys and girls on the follow spots have your color gels and spare bulbs?"

"Yep, yep, yep, yep," from two corners, a stage wing and top center.

"Charles, Anne Marie and Big Daddy the Father, Son, and Holy Ghost are in their places, people. Stand by to rock," Max said.

"Shall Kathy and I take it from here, Max?" Victoria's voice. "Kathy Danuta? Our student stage manager?"

"Er, right. This is the kids' night. Roger, that."

Into her mic, "Kathy, I'm going to check on Charles and Anne Marie. I'll give you the sign when they're ready."

"Thank you, Ms. M."

Victoria was at center stage. Charles peeked out, back-lit from behind the set's bathroom door and waved.

"You're ready, Charles?"

"I think so, ma'am," a quiver in his voice. "Embarrassed to say, I'm a bit nervous. I've never really done something like this."

"A bit nervous is a good thing, Charles. I mean, Brick." She winked.

"Yes ma'am."

In the other wing, Anne Marie sat on a stool checking her lips in a battery-lit, hand mirror. "You look great, Anne Marie. We're going to dazzle them, tonight."

"Fuckin-A," to the mirror.

"I beg your pardon?"

"Oh! Hi, Ms. M."

"I guess I should say, 'Break a leg?'"

"Huh?"

"Have a good time, tonight."

"No problem."

Victoria peeked out at the audience, again. "Ready when you are, Kathy."

Kathy walked onto the set, checked on Charles, asked Anne Marie to kill the mirror and told the booth, "Bring the house down slow, Frankie."

"Roger, that."

"The mayor and superintendent are in the back of the auditorium. Spots two and three, you have them in sight? The two aisles?" Kathy asked.

"Yep, yep."

"Don't blind them. They have to be able to get down the aisles and up to the stage for the presentation. Cue the walkers. Places. Two, three, four, now."

The city's first female mayor started down the aisle. About four percent of the city's voting population, she thought, were African American. Next to no economic pull, and this may be the least political thing she'd done since taking office. Maybe that's why it felt so right. Thirteen percent black, eighty-six percent white, this greater metro area. *This* side of the river, *this* audience, one hundred percent white. Beneath her arm, she carried *The Gazette's* civic unity plaque she would award to the superintendent tonight. Packed house. So, an opportunity for a speech if ever there was one—five hundred in attendance. But, this was the superintendent's night to receive, her night to bestow. Wait. What the...? Well, of course. She looked back over her shoulder as she past the sixth row of unexpected patrons.

Kathy met the mayor backstage right and handed her a wireless mic. They fumbled for a moment. Kathy showed her the power switch.

On the other side of the stage, the superintendent appeared in front of the curtain, and, buoyed by applause, he and the mayor approached each other in their show time strides. They shook hands center stage, and the mayor's mic came on with a *POP*.

"Thank you, ladies and gentleman, and I see families and friends from many of our fine schools. I am a guest here tonight, a guest of our superintendent, our host school and its principal, William Howard Hill, and our play's director, Victoria Merritt." She moved aside and Victoria stepped through the curtain and joined them. "Mr. Hill would be on stage tonight, but he is busy greeting in the lobby. You probably saw him on your way in.

I am also in service of *The Gazette*. As many of you have read, the play the district—the students and faculty—chose for this year's spring production presented challenges to the administration that were previously seen as insurmountable. There were barriers to selection, challenging issues common to all mankind that we as a community sometimes fail to address openly, intelligently and humanely."

The audience rustled in their seats, coughing from the back of the auditorium.

The mayor continued, "*Cat on a Hot Tin Roof*, the Pulitzer Prize winning play by Tennessee Williams, was first performed nearly fifty years ago. The play exposes vulnerabilities in our nature: deceit, greed, the perceived futility of our lives, substance abuse and struggles with identity and sexuality."

"*Sssssssss!*" Hisses streamed from the standing crowd at the back.

William Howard Hill had just stepped from the lobby into the back of the dark auditorium as the, "*Sssssssss,*" and some under-the-breath swearing left the clenched teeth of the underdressed young adults along the back wall. A quick one-eighty and he was back in the lobby and on the phone. As he waited for the deputy to pick up, he admired the five Harley's backed to the curb and sparkling in the glow of the lobby windows. He ought to get a Harley. Come on, pick up, dammit.

The mayor pressed on, "This year's spring production is another example of our community's cultural growth and enlightenment. In recognition, it is an honor to present this plaque on behalf of *The Gazette*." She faced it toward the audience. "You see, here, *The Gazette* article is preserved in its entirety and inscribed above is, 'In recognition of Innovation in Arts and Community.'"

As the applause subsided, the hisses rattled forward from the back. Then, fake coughing and hacking that sounded an awful lot like, "Bull-shit, ass-hole, fuck-you." There were murmurs and shuffling in the audience as patrons stretched, turned then resettled confused.

"Could we have the house lights, please?" the mayor asked.

"Light em up, Frankie. Now! Something's happening out front."

Max had his headset off and was out through the curtains and between the mayor and Victoria as the lights came up. "There's an issue?" He gripped Victoria's upper arm.

"We're good, I think," the mayor said, the mic at her side.

The audience was lit and unsettled. The five large bikers in aisle seven looked to Faye. She nodded. They dropped their programs to the floor. One handed his to the lady in front of him, and they slowly rose. They split up. Three stepped over patrons to the left, "S'cuse, please, s'cuse us," and two to the right.

A few men and women in row six handed off their programs and stood tall. The bikers encouraged them to remain at their seats.

The audience volume increased.

"Ladies and gentlemen, can we take a breath, please?" the mayor asked. "Gentlemen, your seats?"

"You wanna give me the mic?" Max asked.

"Thank you." The mic back at her side, "But, we're still good, I hope."

Coughs and insults continued in the back. The bikers reached the aisles. Fred and Lou glanced up at Max and nodded.

"Francis said there'd be trouble. He said his girlfriend said it's cuz of Charles and the play we're doin," Max said.

"And, you didn't tell me?" Victoria asked.

"What's a kid know?"

Howie was still on the lobby phone. "We're on our way," the deputy said. "Ninety-seconds and there'll be two cars at your curb." Howie hung up and headed back across the lobby to the theater doors as one flew open, and a large, warmed up and firing-on-both-cylinders, Fred Sebastian stepped through. He jerked his head to the side at the student ushers and Howie as in, "Get lost." He held the door open.

A line of twenty-or-so stoic young men, the first two sporting freshly-pummeled noses, and a few women—one sickly thin with a blue Mohawk and a dozen piercings—

filed out of the auditorium past Fred, went straight to the outer doors and exited the building. Bringing up the rear of the march, Fred's brother, Lou, and the three in stars and stripes kerchiefs emerged. One, a walrus of a man, sucked in his gut and edged through sideways.

Red and blue lights fast approached. Two squad cars swept in from two directions locked their brakes and were still blinking and rocking, there by the Harleys, as the deputies popped out. Fred waved them off. "Hey Bobby, Norm. It's all good now, everything settled." The malcontents returned to their rusted-out Camaros, Trans Ams and pick-ups, used their turn signals and observed the speed limit as they left.

"S'cuse, please, s'cuse us," the bikers returned to the seventh row, painfully retrieved their programs from the floor and one from the kindly lady in the sixth row. They wedged into their tiny seats on either side of Faye.

"Cool," Max said. He disappeared through the curtains.

The mayor looked side to side. She and Victoria stood alone. In the fracas, the superintendent had taken the plaque and made his bird—gone. The audience was crackling. "People, please?" the mayor asked. "Please?" She looked up to the booth. "Can we continue?"

"At the top, Frankie, we're starting over."

The lights came down, the audience cooled.

In a single light, the mayor took Victoria's hand and walked to the lip of the stage. She held the mic close to her mouth. "Friends, neighbors, thank you for your decorum, your civility, your support. This is humbling, personally, this moment. I am proud to serve you, our community. I can neither apologize for the people who just left nor the means by which they left." She stared down at the bikers. "I appreciate your intent, but I cannot condone what just happened."

In the dark, the bikers shrugged.

She and Victoria backed to the curtain. "I— Enough, now. We have come to see this young woman's production, and we shall. We thank *The Gazette* for their recognition, and let's enjoy this evening together."

Out in the parking lot chatting with the deputies, and through two sets of fire doors, Howie heard the applause.

And, so it began:

At the rise of the curtain someone is taking a shower in the bathroom, the door of which is half open. A pretty young woman, with anxious lines in her face, enters the bedroom and crosses to the bathroom door.
MARGARET (shouting above roar of water): One of those no-neck monsters hit me with a hot buttered biscuit so I havet' change!

At the end of Act 1, the audience buzzed with electricity. The play was incredible, and how did these kids do it? The end of Act 2 and everyone stayed at their seats, awaiting the curtain to the third and final act.

Final Scene:
(Brick sits on edge of bed. He looks up at the overhead light, then at Margaret. She reaches for the light, turns it out; then she kneels quickly beside Brick at foot of bed.)
 In the blue moonlight raking across them.
MARGARET: Oh, you weak people, you weak beautiful people! – who give up with such grace. What you want is someone to – take hold of you. Gently, gently with love hand your life back to you, like somethin' gold you let go of...

And, there, in the blue raking moonlight—and you-bet-your-ass unrehearsed—Anne Marie slipped her hand into the startled Charles' pajama waist and took hold. The curtain closed slowly.

Stunned.

Frozen.

Dark.

Howie frothed and boiled over in the back of the auditorium. Perfect! Right in front of the mayor, and will it ever end, this goddam Jewess curse?!

Silence.

Francis brought the lights and music up ever slowly with Nat King Cole's *Smile* sounding like it played on a distant car radio.

In the front row center, silhouettes of the mayor and her husband stood. Hers leaned into his and whispered something. They raised their hands and clapped.

The center sixth row stood and joined in, "Yes, sir! Brother Charles!" Sixteen stood applauding. Faye, Fred, Lou and the other three big guys were on their feet, making it twenty-two, "Right on!" Within a few seconds, and perhaps because their shock was overcome with a disproportionate respect for civil propriety, the rest of the audience joined the mayor in applause.

What We're Talking About is Firing an English Teacher

The next morning, during her planning period, Victoria was back in Howie's office. Howie paced. "Is everything around you a mine field? Mortal danger in every direction?" He spun and headed back. "Do you always have to be the tallest nail, your head so far above everyone else's, sticking up and tripping anyone who happens into the room?" He turned back. "As a kid—you played with matches?"

"I—"

"The superintendent stopped by this morning. He witnessed, first hand, the reaction that your play incited. He was fortunate to escape before things got rough, and the deputies arrived. So, he didn't see your play, no, but he sure as hell heard about it. He asked what kind of porn fest I'm running, here, goddam it!"

"Howie, Mr. Hill—"

"The phone hasn't stopped. Principals from other schools, and, oh, aren't they so goddam glib with, 'Heard you're running a tin cat house, Hill.' Calling to twist the knife in my back. Your knife, Ms. Merritt!" The principal perched on the front of his desk, his knees two feet from her chin.

Her execution. She was being fired. She felt a bead of sweat roll down the small of her back. This can't be. Say something, anything. He was stabbing his finger at her, the power of his current forcing her into the gutter. What will I do, what can I do? His voice receded, words out of order, tossed in rage. I must move away, to another town. There was a trace of thick saliva at the corner of his mouth. My only teaching position, and I have no references. He was demanding something. She looked up his nostrils. A single nose hair advancing, retreating—

"Well? Well?!"

"Mr. Hill—Howie—I heard about it from Francis Danuta, from the control booth. I don't know what possessed her. I didn't see it. I was backstage. I've spoken with her. Please." Victoria pushed back into her chair as far from him as she could.

His shirt belly bulged as he folded his arms high on his chest, his wrists poked from his sleeves. "I've been invited to tea this afternoon—the county chapter of the DAR. Tea with the DAR, and I'm the entertainment. Tea and cookies and William Howard Hill turning on a goddam spit!"

"I am so sorry. I'll go in your place. Please, let me go. I take responsibility. You are in no way—"

"No? I'm not?" He was pacing, again, behind his desk. "Your little caravan of sin has parked squarely here!" He slammed his hand on the desk.

"I understand everyone's alarm, really, I do. If we could just— It was a spontaneous indiscretion—for whatever reason—a promiscuous nineteen-year-old, an incomplete young adult. I am as shocked as you."

"You're telling me it wasn't in the script? It wasn't rehearsed?"

"No sir."

"A nineteen-year-old sticks her hand in a boy's pants in front of five hundred people just befuckingcause?"

"I am so sorry."

"Knock, knock. Hi guys. Talking about me?" Marge entered and closed the door.

"What we're talking about is firing an English teacher and permanently expelling a student!"

"Oh, then I've missed a lot." Marge sat next to Victoria. "There's something on your tie, Howie." She pointed.

He looked down and brushed off a hole-punch dot.

"Better," she said. "So," she patted Victoria's thigh, "This must be the teacher, and I fully understand, outlaw that she is. Who's the student?"

Howie dropped into his chair, run out of gas. He turned his back to them. The practice field lay fallow. He scrubbed his face with both palms. The team would be back out there any day, now. Then summer practice, and each year a new chance at the trophy. Football was a great game and dependable; the same each year: the teamwork, the brutal power and speed under the lights. Plays run from the shotgun, the T and I formations, the single-wing... "The newspaper raves over this play. The radio hopes we'll extend it a second week, and the superintendent says we either shut it down, now, or I'll be passing out pudding snacks to six-year-olds."

"Rock and a hard place." Marge winked at Victoria.

He spun back around. In a softer voice, "Can somebody control the girl? Textbook psychopath." He leaned his chin on his hand. In a small voice, "Get her into line, will you?"

"The genie's out of the bottle, Howie. This play is unlike any other student production ever because of Anne Marie and Charles and the daring of this young woman next to me."

He stacked both fists on his desk and lowered his chin to them. An even smaller voice, "She can't put her hand in his pants or whatever she has in mind for tonight."

"We've spoken with her, Victoria and I, individually and together. I think we should get her father involved."

He closed his eyes. "Fuck."

Big Al

Al Delucchi didn't like closing his shop midday. He didn't like having to change out of his white barber's tunic and into civilian clothes. He didn't like the way his wife stood there waiting just inside the bedroom door and dressed like she was going to a funeral and holding her purse in front of her with both hands and checking her watch and frowning. Al didn't like being rushed. "Goddam school, interrupting a man's livelihood." He worked swollen feet into cracked, black and ancient, spit-shined wingtips. They had been his father's. *"Try and be kind, Al."* He heard his father's voice every time he forced his way into those shoes. *"Life is a gift, Al."*

"It's that Hill. Goddam ram-rod-up-his-ass, general on his high horse. Always got a problem, that guy. Little Methodist shit." His wife shifted in the doorway. "Yeah, I know, Rose. I'll keep a lid on it." He hitched his belt and centered his tie. "Anne Marie's your daughter. You ever talk to her? Talk some sense? She was such a sweet little kid." He glanced at the mirror and tore off his tie. "Where's my other tie, the good one?" His wife checked her watch. "Then, about the time the boys start comin round, it's all

over but the shoutin." He flexed both fists at his waist.
"Okay, I ain't wearin a tie, and I don't want to hear a peep
about it, Rose." He pulled on his suit jacket. "We gotta go
there in the middle of the day, and who decides that? How
bout they come here, this time? They got an issue to
discuss. They always got an issue to discuss. Discuss shit
is all they do up there. I got a living to make. How bout we
discuss that?!" Al Delucchi didn't like being told what to
do.

Twenty minutes later, Al and Rose Delucchi huffed up
wide, wet steps past the janitor coiling a heavy hose,
through double glass doors and into the polished tile
lobby of their daughter's school. "Looks like it's trying to
decide if it's the post office or a goddam clap clinic," he
mumbled on their way to the principal. "C'mon, Rose,
keep up, would ya?"

Extra chairs had been brought into Howie's office.
Victoria, Anne Marie and Marge sat stiffly along a side
wall. The two leather barrel chairs directly in front of his
desk were available, the desktop empty, the glass surface
beamed. On either side of the window behind the desk—
the window overlooking the practice field—eagle-topped
staffs hoisted Old Glory and the state flag. William Howard
Hill sat in his buttoned suit jacket, jaw clenched, his
folded, manicured hands on the desk. He was at the ready.
This wasn't his first meeting with Al regarding his
daughter. There had been a few and none were pleasant:
grades, tardiness, unexcused absences, smoking,
drinking, fighting—the girl had a knack for bad choices. It
was like she had a flipping deranged life coach and a
damned good one.

There was a commotion beyond his door. It burst
open. "I'm sorry Mr. Hill," the receptionist called from
behind Al in his large suit and Rose in tow.

"Al, Rose—"

"I don't have much time, Howie. What's goin on?"

"Please, have a seat." Howie stood and offered. "You
know Marge, and I believe you've met Anne Marie's English

teacher, Victoria Merritt?" Al scrunched his face at Victoria and sat. Rose shook Victoria's and Marge's hands, gave her daughter a sympathetic smile and took the chair next to her husband.

"Can I get anyone a water, coffee?" Howie asked.

"I didn't come here for water, coffee, Howie. What is it this time?" He looked over to his daughter. "Anne Marie, you doin your homework?"

She folded her arms and sneered.

"We're in a bit of a bind, here, Al. The school play. It's—"

"Brilliant! I was there. It's perfect. I'm goin again tonight. And, I'd 'a helped with the Hazzard rednecks if Rose wasn't there."

"Yes, well," Howie continued. "There have been some remarks regarding your daughter's, ah, performance—not positive remarks—complaints. There may not be a tonight; there may be no more play. Things have to change, or I may have to do something neither of us is going to enjoy."

"Like, what?"

"Marge?" Howie asked. He pulled a handkerchief from his breast pocket and wiped his upper lip.

They turned to Marge. She stood and came around behind Howie's desk, her hands on the back of his chair. "Mr. and Mrs. Delucchi, your daughter, Anne Marie—" She nodded and smiled to Anne Marie and Victoria. "Anne Marie is quite an actress, a natural method actress, actually. She's immersed in her character, Margaret. She becomes Margaret. That's mostly good."

"So? What?"

"The Margaret that Tennessee Williams wrote is a desperately-longing, passionate and mature woman, not a high school junior. That's our problem."

"What? Anne Marie's not passionate?"

"Oh, you gotta be—" Howie started.

"Please, Howie." Marge placed her hands on his shoulders. She turned her attention back to Al. "Being fully engaged as Margaret plays well, too a point, but there are boundaries, contracts between actors and their audiences, between actors and actors."

"Whatta we talkin about?" Al looked over to Anne Marie, to Howie, and back to Marge.

"Anne Marie has crossed those boundaries by touching her counterpart, the actor playing Brick, inappropriately," Marge said.

"What, inappropriately? Sometimes—I gotta tell you— you people talk like you're on *Masterpiece Theater*, or something." He twisted in his chair and looked over to his daughter. "You touch someone 'inappropriately?'" he asked with his fingers. Anne Marie rolled her eyes and looked out the window. Al faced back to Marge, then shot into Howie, "Can we be more specific about what you and me gotta agree on is inappropriately?"

"Mr. Delucchi, Mrs. Delucchi, you were there. You must have seen Anne Marie—and, yes, otherwise a wonderful performance—you must have seen Anne Marie slide her hand into the other actor's pajamas," Marge said.

Al pushed up out of the chair, "That's what this is about?" He leaned heavy hands wide and deep on Howie's desk and aimed down. "That's your goddam inappropriately?! That she touched him in his crotch? They were in the privacy of their own home. They're married, for chrissake!"

A Confession

Victoria picked the play program from her desk. She moved in cold florescent light past the little coffee maker and turned to the upright files on the counter at the windows. Wind raked the black glass for the length of the room with shot-gunned rain. It had been three days now, and it was like God was making them pay for something, and this time he was really pissed.

June left yesterday in the downpour. She said she was going somewhere without phones or cable. Victoria told her that knowing her had been like a trip to Oz. June said that, just like the story, she'd had it in her all the time and promised to look her up one day. Sometimes it seemed that every way Victoria turned was a false start.

She chewed the inside of her cheek as her fingers combed back and forth through the files. "Ah." She stuck the program into a folder and looked up to his reflection in the glass. "Francis. Sorry, I didn't hear you come in—the rain."

He was soaked. The poor boy was dripping. She watched as he crossed the room, poured a coffee and parked at the corner of her desk. Her eyes backtracked the small puddles to her door. She'd taken a cab these past three mornings.

He told her she looked tired.

She said she was. She said the play had worn her down, that the principal had given her brain damage, though he finally came around with help from Anne Marie's father, and that she sometimes just wanted to stay in bed and pull the covers over her head.

He said, yeah, he heard her. Working on the play had lifted him out of reality for a bit, but he pretty much felt the same way every morning, and that, except for Faye, most of the time he wished he could just disappear.

She said she understood, that the loss his family felt must weigh so heavily, that she would always bear the weight of her father taking his own life and that—

He stood and moved to the rear corner of the room, his back to her, his double profile reflected in the black window, arms wrapped around himself, hands at his shoulders.

He said he'd wanted to kill his father since he was five.

She started to say something, then didn't have words.

He said when he came home that night, the first thing he saw was Kathy upside down on the stairs, her blood everywhere, the Christmas tree smashed and the gun in a smeared puddle of puke. He said it was like a trapdoor opened inside him, and he was afraid he was going to pass out—vomit or shit first, then pass out.

Next, he was standing in the pantry by the cot. Just enough light to make out the snoring body, and it was hot in there—stunk like fucking hell. He was sick and weak, and his eyes were fogged, overflowed, and snot ran down his lip. The gun was slippery and heavy, and he had to use both hands to raise it to the man's chest. He laid it there. Now leave. He had taken a step back, to leave, then didn't because—no—there was more. He stepped up to the cot and said, "I bought you a tie."

No, she thought. Don't.

He lifted the swollen wet hand that hung from the side of the cot, the calloused fingers and palm, the thick, dark, broken nails. He hated that hand. He wrapped it around the gun handle and put one twisted finger on the trigger. He slid the hand and gun up to the man's chin. The barrel scraped and clicked against stained teeth as he guided the gnarled fist and pushed the barrel deep inside. It tried to say something, something indecipherable—something stupid—the mouth with the barrel in the way. Looking down, he saw the man still had his shoes on. He pressed the finger and blew his dad's brains all over the wall.

She stood and took quick steps toward him and stumbled. Her hand found a desk.

He turned to her white. He'd do it again. If he could, he'd do it again.

The Summit

"I told her. Ms. Merritt."

"Yes," Faye whispered.

They were in the Toyota overlooking the valley. Small planes landed and took off far below. Double-celled lights streamed ever slow on invisible arteries along and across the interwoven waters. Twilight traded for dark, and in a micro silver flash, a tiny flock cut through the airport beacon.

"That part's over," she said.

"That part?"

"Yes." She fixed ahead on an early star.

"What's the next part, Faye?"

"The story changes."

The Next Part

Your Turtle's Dead

Victoria hadn't slept. She left a message on the substitute request line. Her head, her joints ached and the nausea.

In the living room the coffee was cold, most of the cup untouched, abandoned on the armrest of the couch. The kitchen, too, cold and barely touched by what little light made it through the rain and the window above the sink. Last night's hair, she sat in her robe at the table, two shoeboxes in front of her, and by mid-morning and a full ashtray, snapshots three-deep covered the table and some on the floor. She lifted another from a box.

Huh, the honeymoon. Who took it? It's a great shot of both of them and sharper than the others. Must have been a steady hand and good camera. God, mom was beautiful, like a celebrity. Grace Baros looked like she could barely keep her feet on the ground, so happy. Dad, too—handsome, proud. Where did James Merritt buy that suit and with what money? His family was so poor, living off the land. She turned in her chair, her back to the little window and held the photo higher and closer. She looked deep into his face, his lips. Was the smile forced? His eyes? She looked for a sign. For something that would say he was, or would be, confused, troubled, would commit the most grievous acts in another seven years. No, he looked happy. If he had attempted to take a life, his own and failed, he would not have been charged with a crime. The authorities would not have been notified. The church would have sympathetically gathered around him—around them—and brought him, the poor dear man, closer to the fold. What a friend we have in Jesus. Sure, until why he was so troubled came to light, until mom found out. Then, he would have been ostracized, and a second attempt would have been successful. For all she knew, that's how it happened. She dropped the photo onto the table.

It had poured that morning before the funeral. The cars parked beneath dripping maples along the gravel cemetery road; Pop's big warm hand holding hers. They stepped out onto sopping grass, and her feet were immediately wet. Mom and most of the women carried their shoes, and Pop's trouser cuffs got soaked. Steam rose around the white canopy, and they all crowded beneath. Up front, between Pop and Mom, she could barely breathe—the flowers.

The men placed the coffin on top of the grave and disappeared to the back of the gathering. Just his name on the stone, "James Merritt."

The preacher was a little brown man with a tiny voice. She wonders, still, who he was—why it wasn't their preacher? His hands were fragile things, the nails bitten down. He opened his Bible but never looked at it. "James was a sinner. He stole, lied, coveted and thought impure thoughts. He shirked responsibility, blamed others for his misfortune, wished evil on people he never met and took the Lord's name in vain. He drank, smoked, committed unspeakable acts and finally rent asunder God's holy temple."

Was he talking about Dad? Her dad?

The preacher stopped, turned his head, coughed the bark of a small dog into his sleeve and aimed black, pointed eyes at them. "All sinners condemned to hell's suffering, lest ye find forgiveness in Christ."

She lit another smoke, took a long drag and laid it on the ashtray.

The authorities seem willing to accept that Francis' father took his life. What is to be gained if I challenge that, as surely I must?

Morality is upheld. That's what.

Really?

Who would question that? I am morally and legally bound. I was witness to a confession of murder.

Says who? The authorities visited the scene right after whatever happened, happened: deputies, the coroner, paramedics. They saw what you didn't. Your expertise? Your degree is in what?

It's not about degrees. It's about taking someone's life, and I was there—there for the confession.

Okay, suppose you're right. If Francis is convicted, he could lose his life—life as he knows it, as you know it. Isabel loses her only son, Kathy, her only brother. Three lives sacrificed, destroyed. Then, you get your cost of living raise and begin a new school year knowing you did the right thing? Very tidy.

And, if I say nothing?

The gutter drains were backed up, and a large puddle lay out front. Traffic sent repeated sprays over the walk and onto her porch, and the school, and the kids, and the principal and the play were washed away. Just the ticks of the stove clock and the little kitchen remained. In front of her, on the table, the small photograph—two lives and their stardust dreams already beginning to fade the moment the image was burned onto the paper. Her hand rested next to the photo, an adult's hand. She stared at it

like it was someone else's, and her thoughts drifted to
Catawissa by the river, and the kids' laughter, and it was
getting late, and her mom was calling. Victoria and her
cousin ran in from the shed and through the back door,
the kitchen all hot and abustle. Her mom wiped her eyes
with her apron, laughing as she filled water glasses from
a pitcher. By the stove, Dad carved the ham. Uncle
Richard poured whiskey into two glasses and sat one by
the ham platter, and from the front room, she heard her
aunt begin to tell another joke. "Come in here, Vi!" her
mom called.

Aunt Vi and Uncle Bernard stumbled into the kitchen
mid-sentence, "...and so, the priest says to the rabbit..."

"And, you let her talk like that from the same mouth
she prays with, Bern?"

"Pray on Sunday, sin on Monday."

"Why didn't he eat the lettuce?" Victoria asked her
cousin.

"Cause he's dead. Your turtle's dead."

"No he's not. And, how do you know?"

"Cause he didn't eat the lettuce."

"He's sleeping."

"He's dead."

"He's not."

The cramp in her stomach brought her back to her
hand. On the lip of the ashtray, just a filter remained, the
ashes dropped in a gray snake. She pushed up, took the
photo down the hall to the dark bathroom and propped it
on the sink. She lit a candle and placed it next to her
mother and father. She reached across the tub, started
the bath and shed the warmth of her robe.

Dreaming as One

Faye and Francis exited the side door of the Turkey Ranch. It was a gem of a day, blue and clear and a break in the collaboration between insects and Fahrenheit. They crossed the gravel lot to the Toyota, rolled the windows down and headed north.

"What if we just kept going?" he asked, both hands on the wheel, three and nine. "Right on up through New York and stayed there on a lake. Like, an abandoned cabin on a lake that froze in the winter, and we barely had enough food to last, but we made it through to spring, and then we dug a garden and raised enough to get us through the next winter, and by then I'd have a job down the road at the old gas station."

She sat with her back against the door and watched the country scroll past his window.

"You know, and we had a big, loopy dog, and we snared rabbits like my Nanna taught, and you're a great cook and all—your bread, that oatmeal cranberry loaf.

We'd sell bread at the farmers' markets to tourists from Arizona and Brazil coming to see the leaves in the fall. All winter I'd carve stuff to sell: ducks, wolves, bears. Polished cherry and walnut carvings, fifty bucks each, maybe sixty-five, depending on the size."

Faye shook her head and smiled.

"Maybe I'd have a beard in the winter. I'm still growing for another year or so. I'd be the tall guy in the trimmed beard with the magic, beautiful wife."

The next few miles passed in his dream until he pulled off onto a dirt road, drove down through the shallow creek, up onto the far bank, into the woods and parked. The car steamed and ticked as it cooled.

"Let's walk," she said.

They followed the long-silent, laurel-choked logging road up the side of the mountain through half-a-dozen switchbacks to the broad flat spine of the ridge. There, the undergrowth gave way, and their feet sank in the moist carpeted shade between the pines. Faye took his hand and wove her fingers into his.

"Francis, you don't know yourself."

"What."

"You should meet yourself. You might like what you see."

"Yeah?"

"You're busy, so busy. Let's stop and look." She pulled him down, and they sat on the bed of long pine needles.

"You told me you wished you had a dog, or played the piano or that you were taller. You are taller, Francis."

"Still can't play the piano. No dog. Can't do much, really."

"You're much taller. Responsible, generous, brave. But, you drift."

"Yeah, I don't seem to be getting anywhere. I mean, at least I have a job and all. And, City College, of course."

Her breathing slowed, and she looked deep into him. "Yes, you've enrolled."

"Development classes, first semester. Get up to speed, maybe."

"You've already passed where most never go. You've been to the edge."

"I don't get—"

"You don't have to get it. We can't get it. The *it* is here, in us, around us, we just can't see it—understand it. Some of us feel it. For now, that's prize enough."

"Like—"

"Yes, Francis, like. Like the sounds we can't hear, frequencies beyond our range—higher, lower. Or, the things we can't see. There are more than the rainbow's colors. Birds see them. Scent, taste, temperature, time— we operate in a narrow band. It's the time part that you saw, there, when you went to the edge. You saw the salvation of your family in a crack in time."

He took a long breath and looked up to the trees. Liquid blue poured through. "That doesn't make anything right."

"Right is another part of *it*, Francis. Right is in you, in us. The village can hide it from us in their laws, their decisions. The village decides for the village. You and I carry right in our hearts." Her eyes washed over his face. She smiled. "You don't have to get it all at once."

They occupied one space. She leaned forward over their crossed legs and kissed each of his palms, slowly, carefully. Sitting back, they stared into each other, and her story folded into his. Around them, all was silent but for the breeze in the pines and, there, a single dove. She reached to his face, and her fingers glided from his hair to his chin. He held her wrists lightly and felt her pulse, and it was then that his name left him—lifted on the wind, drifted above the trees and blown out to sea. His nameless body left behind, his world narrowed and did she push or did he pull? She lay on him, her warm weight and his whole being awake, alive, and he felt every part of her for the first time. Her lips travelled his face, kissed his eyes and he hers. He touched her ear and it was perfect—the bronze curves into itself and smooth. Their hands slid over each other, searching and finding, and buttons and zippers fell away. From over the horizon, and barely heard at first, came the pipes, and already it was too late. Too late to run, to hide. Dust rolled and climbed above distant tree lines, and a slight rumble deep in the earth gained momentum, closer, louder now, and the primal charge was upon them. Ghost horses from storied battles pounded over and around their young bodies. They were thrown onto and into each other in the naked, smoldering wake, she on top and then he. One tried to escape and was drawn back, then the other. The heat in great surges, their rivers boiled, crested and deserted their banks, and they needed water where none remained. Their skin was swollen and red. Bloodied soil filled their noses and mouths, and they shuttered and heaved, and as quickly as it arrived, the conflagration returned to the past and left them for dead.

The breeze was the first to return, cool to their wet skin, then the dove's low mourning song. She slid from him and lay on her back, quiet. He drifted to his side, weak and pulled long needles from her hair.

"It is an old house we will make beautiful," she said.

"What, Faye?"

"Just lie now."

True North

Marge swept into the hotel bar, her raincoat unfurled. "Hi gorgeous." She waved as she cruised past the bartender and found Victoria in the back. "Sorry I'm late. Missed you at school. I thought you were sick."

"Just a headache, really. I'm okay, now," Victoria said.

Long arms, Marge pulled her coat off by the cuffs and slipped into a chair. "Had a session with the Chalupa girl. They always go long. Whiner. If only she could see how great her life is. Then again, it must be such a burden, being born a whiner. Have we ordered?"

"Go ahead, I'm alright."

The bartender stood close to Marge while she ordered and patted her shoulder as he left.

"Badda-bing, badda-boom." Marge watched him return to the bar.

"You like him," Victoria said.

"I need him—the way you need Max."

"What makes you think—?"

"Dearie, your secret is safe with me. Just stop going all drippy every time he's near, okay?"

"I...okay." She blushed and took a sip. "Marge, your sessions are confidential. Your clients trust you with secrets. You maintain their trust."

"Right."

"But, the Chalupa girl? You're okay saying she's a whiner?"

"It's no secret. We all know she's a whiner. She knows we know she's a whiner. Her friends beg her not to whine."

"But, we're professionals. We're under contract, an obligation."

"And discretion." Marge said.

"Pardon?"

"Our discretion is also expected—required."

"But, how are we supposed to know? Where are the guidelines?"

"It's not always black and white. We're just supposed to know when to say 'when.' Follow our inner compass. It's going to vary with each circumstance and with each of us. And, now I guess I should ask?"

"What?" Victoria asked.

"Right."

"Marge, what?"

"Exactly. What's bothering you? Something about confidence, obligation, discretion?"

"No, I'm just not sure I'm getting it. Where I stand in all off that. I'll work it out, I guess."

"Okay, let's talk about something else. How's Francis?"

"Ah! Sorry." Victoria spilled her drink. They soaked it up with tiny napkins until the bartender arrived with a towel.

"Might as well make it two more, handsome," Marge said, and turning back to Victoria asked, "And?"

"And what? There's really no *and*. I mean, he's carrying a terrible weight. They all are: Kathy and Isabel, dealing with a suicide. I mean, what should we expect, right?" Victoria asked.

"Terrible."

"It must tear him apart, continuing as he is."

"Terrible."

"There are things no one should have to do or endure."

"Victoria, what's going on?"

"What?"

Marge leaned across the table and lowered her voice. "Do you have something to get off your chest? There's something eating you, and it isn't the Chalupa girl. What's up with Francis?"

Victoria looked toward the bar, then back to Marge. "I'm afraid he's in trouble."

"Faye? His job?"

"Maybe something to do with his father—that night."

Marge quick glanced at the bar and back. Nearly whispering, she shifted to double time. "Victoria, if he's told you something it's in confidence, and he never told you. Get it? End of story. This is where you shut up. I don't want to hear it. No one should. There was an investigation. It's over. There's legal, and there's right. If Francis was involved—directly—do what's right. That monster nearly killed each of them at one time or other. We're lucky they're still with us. Do you see anguish in their family, in their faces? No, you don't! Have you seen the years and pounds drop away from Isabel, seen Kathy with her friends—stage manager in your play? Yes! Francis and Faye in love? They are at the beginning of their lives together, in love, Victoria, something with which you and I have had little success, that is until I get handsome over there alone and show him what he's been missing." She sat back and nodded to the bartender.

Victoria's ears were ringing.

Turning back to her, Marge asked, "Shall we do a shot?"

He Meets Her Dad

Sweaty palms, Francis rubbed them on the thighs of his jeans, swung out of the Toyota and hiked up the dirt drive. The sun was dropping below the ridge, and dark came on fast in this valley. Huge collapsing woodshed on his right at the top of the drive, and further on up the lot, past the house and at the edge of the woods, the lion. The animal paced in its cage, eyes never leaving Francis. Damn, it was huge! Francis stepped up onto the small side porch. The kitchen door was open, just the screen door between him and, somewhere in there, Faye's dad. Okay, then. He knocked.

Light steps quickly down wooden stairs and Faye appeared, her hands on the screen. He stepped back, and she pushed it open. "Hey. Right on time."

"Hey."

She stalled and cocked her head toward the tree line at the back of the lot. A look of concern, she raised her hand to her ear for a moment, moved past him, down the steps and out to the lion's cage. Gripping the barred gate, she stood with her back to him, motionless.

"Faye?" he asked.

She turned back toward the house, up the steps past him and back through the door.

"What, Faye?"

"Sorry, I'm not sure; something about Jono. Come on, let's meet my father."

He stepped into the little kitchen and rich warm smells of garlic, herbs and fresh-baked bread. The gas stove on the opposite wall was crowded with four sizes of simmering pots, and the miniature table in the middle of the room was like a fancy restaurant's with a white cloth, candles, fresh flowers, set for three and surrounded by mismatched chairs.

She kissed him—a quick peck—took his hand and led him around the table and to the front room entry. She pulled him into the room, dropped his hand and stood at his shoulder. "Dad, Francis is here. Francis, this is my father."

The room smelled like a wet barn. In the dimly-lit corner, the man sat crooked on a straight-backed chair. Large hands like scarred leather gripped the ends of the armrests. His black hair was parted and slicked to one side. He pushed himself creaking and up. Coming into the light his eyes glistened black as coal, and, not yet landed on Francis, stayed on Faye. "Hello, sir." Francis said.

"Hello, sir, and I am Armend. Please call me that, Francis." His eyes moved to Francis, and there was the tattoo: diagonal slashes, like tiger stripes covered one side of his face. Her father took two labored steps forward—they were the same height—and extended his hand. They shook. Armend continued to hold Francis' hand; the grip increased. "Faye is happy when she is with you. She is jewel, this young woman, and she says you are brave man. She says you have love, like I have love."

Francis tried for composure. How much squeeze did this guy have? He felt just the beginnings of sweat. He nodded.

"I trust her. She trusts you."

"Yes sir."

"I will trust you." One final twist of the vise handle, and he released Francis' hand.

"Yes sir." Damn!

"I am Armend, Francis. Come we eat spaghetti. Faye says you like spaghetti."

*

The three high school boys had parked their truck in long shadows a mile up Sulphur Springs Road, pulled a Nike gear bag from its bed and stuck to the cover of the forest as they trotted back down toward the foreign freak's house. Rusty and Bomber Hazzard knew the terrain blind, having been all over that hillside the past six winters setting and retrieving their traps, and the Burton boy had hunted there since he was twelve. They made little sound as they followed deer trails between granite boulders and dense brush.

The Hazzards had conceived the plan. It was the most recent in a series of annoying-to-worse delinquent acts they lived for: flatting teachers' tires, gay-and-race-bashing graffiti, plugging up the school toilets. They were rarely idle.

They crested a final rise, and down at the house there was just a dim light from the kitchen. "Probably a nightlight," Burton whispered.

The boys were in position thirty yards up slope and down wind. A clear shot through the trees and into the exposed cage below. The lion paced, his nose twitched but hadn't located them. Bomber lowered the Nike gear bag to the ground and slowly pulled the nylon zipper. Six hands reached in for the head mount lights, the three black weapons and a box of ammo. The lion picked up his pace, his nose raised. He circled the perimeter of his cage. The boys loaded the weapons.

*

"Francis, more bread." Armend offered the basket. "Faye's bread."

"Really full, sir. Thanks, though." He'd already loosened his belt.

It had been a celebratory meal, a never-actually-warring-but-always-suspicious and coming-together-of-nations meal. The garlic in Faye's bread settled unsettled stomachs, and her thick, rich, wine and veal sauce eased tightly held misconceptions. Around the table in that tiny kitchen, they shared stories, and laughs and relaxed. Then, *Snap!* It came from out back—up the hill.

*

"Lights, on," Bomber whispered. "Fire."

Burton took the first shot. A burst of red from the lion's shoulder. Jono shuddered and turned, his chest heaved, the forest rent with his roar. Another red burst in his neck. More shots rang out: yellow, blue and another red as the boys hit him with paintballs. He circled, muscles straining in rage, and with one swipe of his claws he could have killed all three. He was helpless.

Faye, Francis and Armend raced out of the kitchen and were swept into the frenzy. Intense lights found them and Armend charged the hill like a crippled guard dog. Faye and Francis were stinging targets as they wrestled long sharp corrugated steel from inside the shed and onto the top of the cage. A flash of blue exploded on Faye's ear. She staggered and reeled. The next shot hit her neck. Struck in the face, ribs and thighs, they both hobbled from cage to shed.

Black. Just like that, the lights went out, and the shooting stopped.

Faye dropped to her knees and pressed bloody palms to her ears. From Jono's pacing stare, it appeared the shooters were moving up valley.

Francis kneeled next to her. He cleared her face, checked her palms. He was talking, asking, but she didn't respond. Now Armend knelt by them. Francis vanished for a moment and reappeared with towels and ice. He wrapped her hands.

Armend grabbed Francis' shoulder. "Who does this? Who?"

"Not sure," Francis said. "Probably the Hazzards."

Armend shook him. "What hazards?"

"Rednecks. Whole family of em."

"Why? Why they do this?"

"They hate you."

"Why?"

"You're different."

Father's Day

It was a hot Saturday with black flies swarming in the nearly-visible air that followed Francis from the scattered pile of eighteen-inch oak lengths at the bottom of the driveway up to the ordered and growing cords stacked in and around the ancient three-walled shed. His T-shirt stuck to him. On his way back down the drive for another load, his arms hung like they were held by a single stitch, hands limp at his sides and wood dust stuck to sweat from forehead to knees.

Faye sat on the kitchen porch step and watched. It hurt him every time he looked her way; made something turn painfully deep in his groin—her head bandaged, and her hands fallen in her lap like wounded birds.

"Father's Day, tomorrow," he said.

She nodded.

"Plans?" he asked.

She shook her head.

"I'll bring lunch." He picked four logs from the pile and headed back up to the shed.

Armend came out onto the little kitchen porch with a big jar of refrigerator water and a stack of plastic glasses. Francis could smell him across the distance; the man worked like an ox and smelled like one. Armend sank slowly and sat on the sagging step next to Faye, took off his hat and ran swollen fingers through flat hair. He'd help the man fix those steps. Maybe use some of that lumber stacked behind the shed. He could do the dumb parts, Armend could do the smart parts. "You guys do this every Saturday?" he asked Faye.

A half smile, she nodded.

"Like all year? Winter, too? The ice storms, and all?"

Another nod and a smile.

"Damn. You should have callouses, or something."

"Gloves," Armend said. "She wore gloves."

The Village

There was a tentative tap at her door. Francis peered in through the screen. "Mornin Ms. Merritt?" His voice waivered. She was on her laptop at the kitchen table. "Just stopped to say hi. Passing by, you know? So, this is your place."

"Yes, you've found me and a pleasant surprise."

"Year's over—all of it. Leave the past behind, I guess? Fresh start?"

She stabbed out her cigarette on a saucer. "Fresh start? I'll have a new class, and you'll be in college."

"Yeah, well, I'll be putting that off for a while. Got a promotion at the bakery, and they want me full time. Pay raise and everything."

"Francis, come in here."

He entered and closed the screen door silently.

"Don't let this slip away from you. Do not put off college to work at a bakery."

"I figure I can go to college anytime. Right now, we can use the money. Between Mom and me working, we'll have more than we've ever had. We might fix up the kitchen."

She pushed the laptop aside, placed her hands flat on the table and sighed. "This is how it continues to unravel?

Your life for a new kitchen? Come here and sit."

Hands behind him, he entered the kitchen and leaned back against the wall. His eyes did a nervous lap of the room. He pulled out the chair across from her, his expression flat.

"You must recognize that you are at another crossroads, Francis, and I'm beginning to think we're players; actors in someone else's play. That it has all been loosely written for us."

"Like, how—?"

"Do you wonder at fortune—at the few classmates who seem to glide effortlessly through school? Others seem, come what may, to struggle in all directions? The Hazzards and their friends: scheming, cutting corners and causing mayhem with every move; their cruelty to that lion—Faye?"

He pushed back from the table, crossed a leg and picked at his cuff.

"Perhaps their community service will sober them, but it's not a good bet. There are those who seem predestined to chaos and failure," she said.

He switched legs and stared past her at the couple in the snapshot on the refrigerator.

She flipped her lighter open, then closed. "Yes, like my father—and yours—and now you."

"I wasn't thinking that."

"Francis, there is something we must do."

His shoelace was coming undone. He reached down and snugged it up.

"Francis, can we discuss something?"

He coughed, dry. "What?"

"Do you trust me?"

"Yeah, sure." He untied and retied.

"And you believe I want you have a healthy life—a fulfilling life?"

He nodded and switched legs. He looked uncomfortable, as if the chair was too small, too close to the table. He walked it back an inch.

"Part of you is charming innocence: your fresh eyes on this old life. That's on the positive side. Another way of looking at it is that there is a disconnect in you—with life, with scale. One cannot equate a new kitchen with a college education and the rest of your life. And, I wonder at the scale you ascribe to what you told me."

"What?"

"You took a life, Francis. Have you heard that in your head today and every day for the past six months?"

He dropped his foot to the floor, crossed his arms and stared at her.

"There's a one-word answer to that," she said.

He glared.

"There are consequences—moral and legal. You can't—"

"No, you can't!" He launched from the chair. "You don't know, and you can't judge!"

She took a deep breath.

He turned to leave.

Easy, easy... "There are a couple Pepsis in the refrigerator," she said. "For us. Do you mind? I'd like a glass and ice with mine, please."

He stalled. He thought he'd be like, have a nice day and see ya later. Instead, he crossed the kitchen, squeezed behind her and opened the fridge. He held the door open and stared. A few seconds, a gurgle and the fan motor came on. Behind him, the front door closed, and Ms. M returned to her seat, her back to him. He heard the nervous metallic flip of her lighter. Milk, eggs and orange juice in a small bottle with a green plastic lid. Tupperware with leftovers. Stuff in the meat tray, green things in the vegetable drawer, and mustard, jelly and other stuff in the door. Olives. He hated olives. She keeps her bread in here. Mom said you're not supposed to do that. He placed the Pepsis on the counter, pried the ice tray from the freezer and closed the door.

"Small cabinet over the toaster," she said.

He set two tall glasses on the counter, twisted the ice tray and sent cubes flying across the surface and into the sink.

"Did you save a couple?" she asked.

She was quiet as he dropped a few into the glasses, poured—*fizz*—waited and poured the rest, slid the truant ice cubes into the sink and returned to the table.

"Thank you," she said.

Head down, hands in his lap, his glass on the table in front of him, he nodded.

"Have you told anyone else what you told me about your father?"

"No."

"Do you want to?"

"No."

"Francis, this isn't just going to go away. You are carrying a burden that will eventually cripple you. Can we—?"

"No. Just leave it alone. I'm sorry I told you."

"I won't do or say anything without you. But, I think we should talk with someone. We can go to a lawyer and discuss options."

"There aren't any."

"Francis. There's a lawyer who specializes in juvenile—"

"Options. There aren't any options."

"We don't know that. I propose we find out instead of hiding and guessing for the rest of our lives."

"The village does what's right for the village."

"I'm sorry?"

"I don't want to talk about it, and you don't have to worry. This isn't about you."

"Francis where are you getting this? The village?"

"The sheriff and the courts, and all—the laws aren't to protect me. They're for the village."

"They exist to set an agreed upon standard of well-being—individual rights and protections," she said.

He stood and turned to go. "You don't know. Just leave me alone, okay?"

"Francis, please."

He was in the front room and on his way out. "I gotta get to work, and talking to a lawyer is for your benefit, not mine."

"Will you think about it? Think about you and me talking with someone? It doesn't mean we commit to anything. We'll just get some advice. Think about it?"

He left the door open. The screen door slammed.

The bakery was its own reality: its own rules, quotas and urgent noise. For a while, it replaced the rocket attack in his head. He pulled another folded box from the stack, opened it, picked up the tape gun, taped the bottom, dropped the box onto the platform next to the conveyor and caught up with the packages of hotdog rolls moving past. Twenty-two, twenty-three, twenty-four and he hardly had to count. The rolls nearly found their way into the box on their own. He spun the box to the side, gave it a shove and it disappeared through the sealer-labeler.

Cripple him? That's what she said? This was going to eventually cripple him? Because he was carrying a burden? She thought he was sorry—sorry for the rest of his life? Was he? Did it look like he was? Hell no!

Like, okay. Yeah. He knew. He knew what was up like nobody knew, cause they weren't there, right? So, now, he was gonna be crippled by this? Cause he didn't talk to a lawyer? So, if he talked to a lawyer, then it would be all, "Do you swear to tell the truth?" And he'd be, "You can't handle the truth." And he'd be all Jack Nicolson in *A Few Good Men*, but he wouldn't get off, because this wasn't Code Red. See a lawyer? No way, was what *he* was thinking. Ms. M could take a hike, was what he was thinking. Crippled for life? Talk to a lawyer? He really friggin doubted it. He grabbed another box, taped the bottom and the packages fell in: one, two, three...

The Other Death Sentence

The following Saturday, Victoria went to a baseball game: a minor-league game, local team—*The Cutters*. It wasn't that she loved baseball, well, except for *The Yankees*. Her Pop had been such a *Yankees* fan in the Mantel/Maris era, and it had rubbed off. Mickey Mantle's *Yankees* held a place in her imagination right up there with Amelia Earhart and the Declaration of Independence, Harriet Tubman and the U.S. Constitution, but, baseball in general, she couldn't care less. No, it wasn't because she loved baseball that she went to a game. It was to talk to a lawyer.

She had called the law office of McEuen and McEuen, Criminal Defense Attorneys. Their billboard atop the grand old hotel on the other side of the river indicated that one of their areas of expertise was, "Juvenile Defense." Perched ten stories in the air, they were a good-looking pair of attorney's, the McEuens. Maybe brother and sister, she thought, but more likely husband and wife: Joel and Stephanie.

Her call had been discouraging until Joel McEuen himself finally got on the phone. The receptionist had been explaining that the McEuens work state wide, had very busy schedules, and their first available opening for consultation was six weeks out. Victoria had persisted.

Couldn't she just squeeze ten minutes in, perhaps during a lunch?

"Miss, there are only so many hours in a day and our office is—"

"I'll talk to them, Tiffany," a male voice. "Joel McEuen, here."

Victoria explained that she just needed informal advice at this point, maybe ten minutes of his time.

"*Cutters* game Saturday. We have two seats. Steph can't make it. Section three, second row, one and two. Go to Will Call. See ya there."

She was going to a *Cutters* game.

It was her first time at a serious ballpark. Taking half steps, she shuffled along in the crowd, through the turnstile, down the hallway, up the stairs, past the concessions and souvenirs to the sign, "Section Three," up more stairs, through the archway and wow! She stood for a moment, there at the top of Section Three and felt the exhilaration of space, color and scale: the air was fresher, and it was as if she hadn't known breathing before this with the great expanse of brilliant green laced with the groomed base paths, and above her a great, blue dome of cloudless sky. Then, *Crack!* Batting practice. Below her one of *The Cutters* sent a white missile arcing high over the center field fence. Fantastic! She stepped her way down the aisle stairs to the second row and seat number two.

She would not betray Francis' trust. She would speak only in generalities, no names, all hypothetical. She was a high school teacher, after all, had many students, and she could be inquiring on behalf of any one of them, right? Or, perhaps none of them—just inquiring for her own edification.

"Whoa, pardonez moi." He was white—blond and white and a maybe one-time athlete now comfortably retired. Diced onions landed in her lap.

"Damn, sorry about that. Here, I have napkins." The guy slid a huge beer into the seatback holder, balanced two hotdogs in one hand and pulled a wad of napkins from the back pocket of his shorts.

She took the napkins and brushed the onions from her slacks.

"Joel McEuen." He sat and stuck out a hand. In his other hand the hotdogs hovered in the aisle. "And, you're Victoria."

"Yes. I am pleased to meet you Mr. McEuen."

"It's Joel."

"Ladies and gentlemen, please rise..."

They reseated. "So, I guess we have some things to talk about, something about a kid?"

"Yes, I—"

"How bout we do that after the game. Right now, we eat and drink. Can I get you a beer, by the way? I'm having another. We'll cheer *The Cutters*, yell at the umpire—I hope you're not the sensitive type—then, we can talk." He drained his cup and was on his feet. "Really, what can I get you?"

Joel was right about the yelling. Victoria was taken by his bottomless and creatively-expressed criticism of the umpires and coaches. In the hours that followed, she was also convinced that if this was the best source to consult regarding juvenile rights—juvenile justice—she wouldn't be needing much consultation, after all. The ushers made regular stops at their row and once brought security by. Nine innings later, and Joel rung out by another *Cutters* loss, he walked her to the edge of the parking lot beneath the bridge and stared across the creek.

"Our weeks can be frustrating—the injustice, the helplessness. We bust our asses doing what's right for our clients, but things aren't always decided the way you'd expect. Some judges have some wiggle room, some laws don't. There's little sense to it. I've seen decisions fly in the face of everyone's interest. Everybody loses. *The Cutters* games are my me time, my catharsis—meditation. Like, 'Om Mani Padme Hum,' and that was a strike you blind sonofabitch."

Behind them, the last of the cars were leaving the lot.

"Joel, you said our talk would be in strict confidence."

"Absolutely."

"Anything I say to you goes nowhere?"

"Right."

"No matter what?"

"As long as it doesn't indicate you intend to do harm to yourself or others." His gaze followed a tandem trailer as it crossed the bridge above them.

"What if it concerns something in the past—months ago?" she asked.

"Dead."

"I'm sorry?"

"Goes nowhere." He watched as the truck headed north.

"Something major?"

"Even if it was something major—like murder one or two—and the dust is settled, there's nothing requiring me, or you, to tell anyone about it, ever," Joel said. "In fact, talking to you now, I'm already bound by client-attorney privilege." He scratched his head and turned to her. "But if it was something major, and the DA got wind and decided to make something of it, well, then there'd be the jury, and all."

"But, he's a minor!"

"Oh? Well. You're in William Penn's Sylvania, and when it comes to capital crimes, juveniles are tried as adults. Somewhere down the line there'll be that jury, and even if we do the best defense job as seen on TV…" He pulled a coin from his pocket and flipped it. "It can come down to this.

Whoa, come over here." He dropped to his haunches. "You gotta see this."

She crouched next to him.

"I flipped it fair and square, and what do you see?"

"It's on the ground."

"It's on its edge," Joel said. "Stuck on its edge in all the confusion and noise. Anyone call it?"

"Okay, I see what you're saying about gray areas." Victoria said.

"Oh, that's not what I'm saying." He pointed his finger close to the coin. "Enter the jury. If the verdict is 'guilty' the coin's always going to end up on the same side, and there's nothing you, or I or the judge can do about the sentencing. The touch of a jury's finger and that's that."

"What's that?"

"Mandatory life without parole. State law, no questions, no wiggle room."

Victoria stood up. "He's a kid!"

Joel picked up the coin, placed a hand on the ground for balance and stood. "Yeah. Sucks, huh? P-A has more juveniles serving life than any other state. About five hundred, and counting. The other death sentence, 'Death by Incarceration.' Another scary fact? Juveniles are more likely to get life without parole than adults who commit the same crime. So, what are we talking about here? Not that you have to say."

"We're not talking about life without parole," Victoria said. "I don't think we're really talking about anything at all."

They walked down to the water's edge. Joel picked up a stone, leaned back and side-arm skipped it to the opposite bank. They watched the creek flow on its own for the next full minute.

Hands in his pockets, Joel sighed, turned and started back toward the stadium. He spoke to the sky, "Okay, then. You got a ride?"

She didn't turn around but said to the creek, "I take the bus."

"Right." He continued across the lot. "Nice meeting you, and cool for me the quarter landed on its edge. Makes me look like a goddam prophet."

Cold and Damp

Victoria woke the next morning in the dark. Max snored. She pulled on heavy socks, wrapped in his wool hunting coat and sneaked out to the bathroom, then downstairs. The sneaking probably wasn't necessary, given the volume of the snoring, but she needed some down and alone time for steeping tea and thoughts. She lit the gooseneck lamp on the kitchen table, it's metal shade ensuring light would fall only onto the table's surface; the rest of the kitchen cast in eerie shadows. She put water on for tea. She plucked the Sunday paper from the front step and dropped it onto the table. Despite summer, Max's kitchen was cold and damp—the whole house: nineteenth-century stone, a deserted farm. He was more-or-less a squatter.

She poured the water and returned to the table with her cup. She should be sure of herself before confronting him: her love, his love, their love. He hadn't said it, that he loved her—the actual words. She knew he liked her, and he was loving, and they made love. But, he hadn't said it. If she asked him directly, he might say, "Of course," or something more evasive, "You have to ask?" But, she had to know. She had to know like he knew.

"Hey, coffee on?" He stepped a bare foot down into the distressed kitchen. Boxer shorts and a sweatshirt. "Nope, no coffee on. Damn, Vic." He rattled through the cupboard and a drawer and got it going. "There. G'morning."

Daylight had arrived.

"Good morning." She didn't think she could ask. Not now. But, there was something else.

He straddled a chair across from her and grabbed the funnies section.

"Max, there's something I want to say. But, I don't know if I should."

He flipped the paper open, a barrier between them. "Why shouldn't you?"

"It's the kind of thing that wants to be kept secret, but I feel compelled."

"You're married," he said from behind the paper.

"No."

"He's a billionaire. Been gone the past three years developing a hotel in Dubai. Comin home soon, and that's why you gotta tell me." He looked out from behind the paper. "No, wait, he's not a billionaire, only a millionaire, and he's just back from sailing around the world. Gets here tomorrow. He's—"

"Max."

His head went back in the paper. "Vic, we all got secrets. Be a burdensome thing if we all shared them. I mean, that's why they're called secrets, cause we don't blab em around."

"Blab. There's a word. Then I guess I should keep it to myself rather than be accused of blabbing."

"Right."

"I don't blab."

"Of course not."

"That's an ugly word, Max."

"Go figure."

She reached across and snapped his paper.

"What's your secret?" he asked.

"I'm not going to tell you."

"Fine, then."

"Fine." She stood, went over to the sink, her back to him. "It's Francis."

"It's your secret or his?"

"It's his, but he's told me and it's a burden."

"And, now it has to be my burden, why?"

"Because you help me by listening. Because we're a couple—in love, and you can help me with this." She went back to the table and sat.

A dark winter's silence dropped into the space between them. Max closed the paper and laid it next to the lamp. His face, his body, took on unfamiliar weight: the same Max, but painted by a different artist. "'This' being you wrestling with the devil?"

"Yes."

He stood, went over to the coffee maker and poured a cup.

"I think Francis killed his father," she said.

He stirred his coffee, threw the spoon into the sink and, back still to her, took a sip. "Why?"

"The man was a monster. He repeatedly abused—tortured—all of them: the kids—Francis and Kathy—and Isabel, his wife."

"No. Why? Why do you think that?"

"He told me."

"Why?"

"Why did he tell me?"

"Yeah."

Had she asked herself? Would he have told his mother, Marge, his priest? Why had he told her? "I…I'm not sure why."

"Huh."

She Comes Clean

Francis drove them out through the neighborhoods and across the humming steel bridge. It was at the end of her sleepless Sunday night that Victoria had called him and asked for a ride to Max's place. Marge was already at Rehoboth Beach for the summer, or she would have asked her. And, if Max had a phone, she might have called him directly. Until last weekend he was at her place, or she at his, every night, and last Sunday he had taken her home and dropped her off in silence, and now she hadn't seen him for a week, and she had to talk this through with Max, and where he stood regarding her and them, and she had to do it today because—

Because she was getting in deeper by the minute, and fantasies flying all over the place, and wildly imagining their future, and her all-or-nothing-at-all bank of emotions overdrawn, and was she just doing this to herself and blindly in love for the first time and joyous at every moment together, and was she in love with him or the idea of him, or in love with love, and did it really matter in that, for whatever reason, she was falling through thin air, and fully exposed, and vulnerable and terrified?

"You're pretty quiet, Ms. M." He signaled a turn.

She looked out her passenger window. "Yes, I'm a bit overwhelmed, at the moment."

"The class thought there might be something going on with you two. Some thought it was Ms. Sweeny, some thought it was June." He slowed the car as they slipped into a foggy bottom.

She turned front. "We've been seeing each other."

"Sorry, didn't mean to pry. Must be hard, though, not having a car."

"Yes."

"Kind of a long drive for him every day, seventeen miles," he said.

"It's rent free."

"We could own our place in another couple years. Then we're in like Flint, as Mom likes to say."

"Turn here. Left. 'Flynn.' It's, 'In like Flynn.' Your mother's given up on college?"

"No, we just decided to take care of a few bills first."

"How does Faye feel about that? Right at the fork."

"Been pretty quiet. Hasn't said one way or the other."

"She nearly aced the SAT. She'll be leaving in another year."

"Local. Says she's staying local."

"Because of you?"

"And her dad. We're good, now, me and Armend."

"Armend?"

"Her dad. I like him. He's teaching me stuff— carpentry."

She glanced at him then back out her window. They were on the river road, fifteen feet above the water. On the other side of the river, green rows of young corn stuttered past.

Awkward silence in the front seats, it occurred to her to tell Francis she'd talked to a lawyer. She should. She turned his way for a moment, then back to the window.

"Francis, I've talked with a lawyer."

He flipped a quick glance at her. He took both hands off the wheel, scratched his head, hammered both fists on the wheel and checked his mirror. The car swerved. He took them off the road and slammed the brakes in the dirt.

"Fuck!"

He threw the door open, got out and busted a new trail through the brambles, over the bank and down to the water.

Across the tops of the weeds, she saw his head as he paced. He talked to himself. Now what? She unfastened her belt, unlocked her door and stepped out.

"Leave me alone!" he yelled.

She started toward him and got caught in the stickers. "Francis."

"The investigation's over. Everything's over, and you keep bringing it up. Shit to make you feel better, and shit that'll send me to prison! What the fuck's the matter with you?" He picked up a rock.

"The lawyer doesn't know who we were talking about. Your name never came up."

"It's a small town. You think he doesn't know exactly who you're talking about? This is so screwed!" He reared back and sent the rock streaking over her head.

She ducked and quick-stepped back. "He is bound by attorney client privilege, and no specifics were discussed."

He picked up another rock, measured its weight and turned it in his hand. "Who else did you tell?"

"I..." She edged back closer to the brambles.

"Who?"

"Francis, I know that I've meddled where I shouldn't have. And, now, looking at it now, you were right. Talking to a lawyer really *was* for me."

"Who else?"

"Max."

Crack! The rock struck her knee. "Uhh!" She fell to the ground and gripped her leg.

He looked around for another rock.

"Francis, stop. You can't stone me to death."

"You told a lawyer, you told Max. What the fuck? Who else? Why'd you tell Max? Geesh!" He found another rock.

"Max didn't believe me. He doesn't take me seriously."

"Yeah? Well you're doing some serious damage to my life." He cocked the missile.

"No, Francis." Her hand went up. "Wait." She worked to stand. The rock hit like a shot, the same knee and she fell to her side. "Unngh!" She cried, "Francis, no!"

He stood over her, fists clenched.

She couldn't breathe.

"You weren't there when he murdered us! You weren't there when he beat mom with the kitchen phone and slammed her into the wall. You weren't there when he tried to strangle me and mom screaming and hanging off his back. You weren't there to see my sister all busted up and her blood all over the wall and stairs and all the other times he murdered us! He killed us and, YOU WEREN'T FUCKING THERE!"

She lay curled on the river stones. No more rocks were thrown, and, when her tears had stopped and she had calmed, she was alone. On her hand by her face, she watched a large black ant climb on, cross her flesh and disappear into the wet stones on the other side. Her knee throbbed and her hip, her face and shoulder ached. Stiff and parts not working right, she collected herself, forearms on the smooth rocks, she worked her way up and hobbled to her feet. Leg numb, knee swollen shut, she fell into the thorns twice getting up to the road. The car was gone.

Stinging scratches on her hands and face, numbness wearing off, the pain drummed up her leg and demanded full attention. Okay, then, teeth clenched, slow and easy. Step at a time.

Francis was drained. He'd made it less than a hundred yards up the road when he had to stop to throw up on the macadam. Cold sweat, like coming to after passing out, he'd lost his shit with her, and it was scary. It had just hit him, like, *Bam!* and it was in his chest, and his arms, and his head, and he hardly knew what was happening, and he couldn't stop. He wouldn't— It wouldn't...happen again. Right? He wiped his mouth with the back of his hand. Was he...? No. He wouldn't be like him.

From behind the wheel, he stretched and pulled a roll of paper towels from the back seat, wiped his eyes on his sleeves, tore off a towel, wiped the snot from his upper lip and blew his nose. Why'd she keep doing this, keep wedging into his life? Saw a lawyer? She's the one got this whole thing going: keeping him after class, meeting before school, checking his goddam homework, grilling him about fucking college, and her cookies, and coffee, and talking about her dad, and being a friend, and...

He looked up to the mirror—red eyes—and back there, from around the corner, she came. Slow and crooked. He'd hurt her. Hurt Ms. M. He backed the car slowly and stopped. He leaned across and opened the door.

He Wonders What a Place Like This Would Cost

Francis pulled back onto the road and drove in silence. Victoria replayed the last twenty minutes, the air tight between them, and she could tell he was reliving it, too. What to say? That they should start over—that she would wait for him to come back as a friend—when he was ready? No straight lines here. Twisting roads and they went into, then away from, the raking morning light. The car slowed, and they slipped into a fog-smothered valley. Flat eyes at the windshield, she shifted her position and grimaced. "Right at the store."

They drove past hundred-year-old barns and depressed cottages by the creeks, over a single lane bridge and followed cutbacks up steep hills, one topped with a small church, naked and alone on a Monday morning. They dipped into deep bales of cotton fog in wooded hollows and, here, the road narrowed, the paved surface eroded and the little car came loose on dirt and gravel.

"This is it. Turn between the posts."

Francis crept the car down a puddled, overgrown lane wound between ancient elms. Fifty yards in, they passed a stone barn crumbled nearly to its knees. There, the ruts split off and led beneath the barn into a wagon stall, beyond which a narrow path led through tall feral grass to the recently-braced front porch of what had once likely been a rich and vibrant two-story home.

"Stop here. His truck's gone." Her voice had lost its tone. She raised to one side, made a small animal sound and twisted her way out of the Toyota.

Francis rolled his window down and turned off the motor. Hands on the top of the wheel, he watched her limp toward the house until she was hidden by the weeds. She was hurt. He'd hurt her, and now she was afraid— something about Max. There was no undoing. Like, say he was sorry? That didn't cover it.

He sank into the seat and closed his eyes. They burned. He took a deep breath, and he could smell the place: the rotted worm-drilled wood, musty bird and rodent nests in the barn, the moss-green wet rock walls and a light breeze sliding sideways through the elms. A shift in the wind and over the roof and the salt dry ash of a thousand fires in the chimney hearth drifted down. He imagined holiday feasts, and children's laughter, and could he do that? Be a father? A good one? Him and Faye, this house? Fix it up a little at a time. Maybe just live in part of the house at first: kitchen, bedroom, bath. He wondered if it had a bath—maybe an outhouse? The place must have water though. So, there's probably an indoor toilet. He wondered what a place like this would cost?

Victoria followed the narrow path up to the house and used both hands on the rail as she stiff-legged up spongy steps and, again, took her chances across the rickety porch floor. She made her way down the length of the house from window to window, placed her hands to the glass and scanned empty rooms. She stepped off the porch and, fleeting hope in hurried breaths, stumbled around to the side and peered into the kitchen where she had boiled water for tea, and he had brewed coffee, and she once made them breakfast, and they laughed at her battered eggs, and they shared the morning paper, and he always read the funnies first, and last Sunday he said not to blab, and the gooseneck lamp and the table and chairs were gone.

It is a New School Year and...

They tumble into her classroom and flit, flutter and chirp like wrens finally landing in a semblance of order in the rows and aisles of solemn desks: thirty-two students she will come to know over the course of the year, most in new shoes and smelling like JCPenney. At her desk in the corner, Victoria Merritt sits in loose earth tones, comfortable shoes and an open collar.

The students fidget, fuss and coo. Ignoring her, they squeal in jibes and laughter. She watches a gaggle of bruised and ruddy boys in the back corner hoist their short sleeves and compare triceps. A few kids, perhaps new to the school, sit tense and quiet.

Some of their brothers and sisters were in her class last year. That class had become a family fused by laughter and sorrow. Some were seniors now, some have gone to college, a few have moved away, one has dropped out of school and one would soon be taking time off to have a child. Her gaze strolls the aisles. Each face a new

story. Each its own dreams, achievements and failures—
secrets and betrayals, large and small. And still they
dance. On weekends, they gather, and laugh and dance.

One, a small pale girl with unevenly chopped hair and
elfin features, sits stone still behind Francis' sister, Kathy.
Hands folded on her desk, neck tense and flushed, the girl
stares out the window. Victoria watches the quick shallow
breathing. She is in no hurry to begin.

ACKNOWLEDGMENTS

You can't just make this stuff up, and I am grateful for those who have helped and encouraged me: Camille Minichino will never know how the crumbs fallen from her table sustain me daily. Jo Mele unlocked plot issues with a few quick turns, the nonchalance of an Italian cook and in lovely humor. Sarah Brennan, Jane Caldwell and Mitch Allen suffered through early drafts and suggested more focus and less baggage ("Get rid of at least two Popes and the Chinese stripper."). Ammi Keller tore down my scaffolding, showed me how crooked my house was and put me back to work. Joel McDermott's legal advice took Victoria to the ballgame, and Jason Wallace honed the edges of punchlines. Phil Laird, Robert Matthews, Howard Rappaport and Jalmeen Kaur had questions and comments in late drafts that pushed me out of my own way. Caitlin Brennan provided bump starts at numerous stalls, and Jane Burton was there through the beginning, middle and end as confidant, acid-bath critic and my love. Thanks, Craze.

ABOUT THE AUTHOR

H J Brennan has filled some of life's everyman slots: field picker, grease monkey, garbage man, barn builder, steel worker, bartender, art teacher and creative director. For six years, while writing his debut novel, *Fathers' Day*, he worked in a bicycle shop. He has attended Kutztown, Temple and Stanford Universities and lives in Northern CA with his wife and two daughters.

June & James
A Love Story
by
H J Brennan

Venice Beach, 2015

There are things that'll put a hole in you. Drop you where you stand. If you make it back to your feet, you probably don't want to talk about it. You put it behind you, give it some time, throw on a fresh shirt and things will get better. It's the story you tell yourself over and over and the weeks pass, and the years pass and maybe you come to believe it. But you still don't breathe right.

Maybe your life has been satisfactory. You've managed well and things are pretty much as you planned: all the right schools, jobs, a home at the coast. Maybe you've actually done the things on your resume. Or, maybe you're more like my neighbor Erskine who's blown HR directors into the weeds with his fabricated accomplishments: Rhodes Scholar, Navy Seal, co-inventor of the SIM card—all glaring bullshit, but he stared them down and got away with it.

I wasn't always sixty. I was young once—vital. It's my story. If I were to tell it, I'd make it sound like a double-feature matinee with free popcorn, the best ride at the carnival and maybe you'd wish you lived like me. I'd probably exaggerate the good parts and take a wide path around the parts long buried. I'd tell it as if I was still there and put you in the moment as I saved the child, won the prize, fell in love.

There's not time here to tell my whole story: parents, siblings, jail, the dried-up jobs and romances—leaves scattered with the wind. But the cherry pickings could make a story. Bite into the low fruit—the times I got away with it, and some that I didn't—like that first night with June.

Maryland, 1990

Strange, to be alone with her, June and me at this table. She looks somewhat like the June we see on the job every day, but in candlelight and through a different lens. Mid-twenties, crystal clean, detailed lips, coal-black eyes and her movements echo—like a dream.

Her hands are big. She's cleaned them up, must have really scrubbed and clear-polished her short nails. Her broad, dark wrists are bangled in silver hoops. Her ears too, in not-much-smaller hoops. The sweat and musk are gone. She's sweet and dancing light patchouli—hair freed from the daily bandana, and damn, June's got a lot of hair: tall, wide and black.

She reached for the basket and chose a roll. The knife jumped into her hand, and she drove it into the butter. Bread raised to her mouth showed light scars and live nicks on her knuckles. Glossed lips parted. June has strong, bright teeth.

We were to have been four tonight. I did something I can't remember to piss off Margaret—my wife—and there I go again, and she won't be talking to me for days; she bailed at the last minute. So, when June showed up at the door all smiles, like Rousseau's Technicolor gypsy in layered skirts and hyper focus, Margaret wouldn't even come out to say hello.

"I'm going, now, Margaret!" I called to the bedroom door. "Back by midnight!"

Made in the USA
Middletown, DE
15 April 2018